WHOSE FAULT?

WHOSE FAULT?

RYAN D. PATTERSON SR.

XULON PRESS ELITE

Xulon Press Elite
2301 Lucien Way #415
Maitland, FL 32751
407.339.4217
www.xulonpress.com

© 2021 by Ryan D. Patterson Sr.

All rights reserved solely by the author. The author guarantees all contents are original and do not infringe upon the legal rights of any other person or work. No part of this book may be reproduced in any form without the permission of the author. The views expressed in this book are not necessarily those of the publisher.

Due to the changing nature of the Internet, if there are any web addresses, links, or URLs included in this manuscript, these may have been altered and may no longer be accessible. The views and opinions shared in this book belong solely to the author and do not necessarily reflect those of the publisher. The publisher therefore disclaims responsibility for the views or opinions expressed within the work.

Unless otherwise indicated, Scripture quotations taken from the King James Version (KJV)–*public domain.*

Paperback ISBN-13: 978-1-6628-2249-0
Ebook ISBN-13: 978-1-6628-2250-6

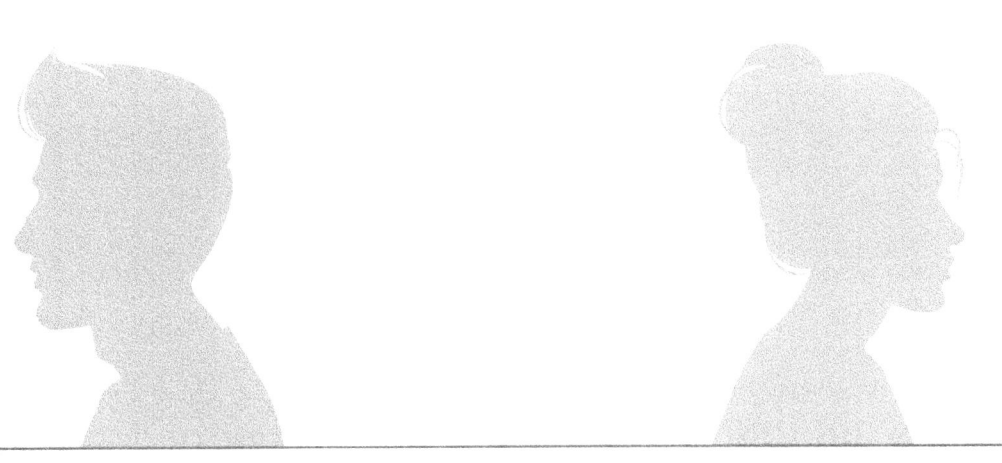

Table of Contents

Chapter 1 1
Chapter 2 4
Chapter 3 18
Chapter 4 25
Chapter 5 29
Chapter 6 42
Chapter 7 45
Chapter 8 52
Chapter 9 56
Chapter 10 61
Chapter 11 72
Chapter 12 80
Chapter 13 93

CHAPTER 1

Abbey

Abbey walked out the back door and checked the thermometer... eighty degrees. She gazed at the leaves on the big oak tree and noted an absence of wind.

Today is a good day to just relax. The kids are gone, and Doug is golfing. I can finally finish this novel. Abbey grabbed a folding lounge chair and moved it closer to the swimming pool. Grabbing her towel, she kicked off her slippers and sat down. The rays from the sun warmed her skin. Her muscles relaxed. Eventually, she became drowsy.

Lying the book on her chest, she had just given into the drowsiness. A loud noise from inside the house startled her.

"Mom!" Julia yelled.

A few seconds passed as Abbey blinked and tried to pull herself out of the warmth-induced fog.

"Mom! Are you home?" Abbey's daughter bellowed the words as only the young can do.

Abbey jerked and watched as the book slid off her body and plopped into the swimming pool.

WHOSE FAULT?

"Outside." Her mouth had gone dry, and the words came out in a croak. *Gotta find some water.*

Julia opened the door and slammed it behind her. As she turned around, Abbey noticed tears streaming down Julia's face.

"What's the matter?" Abbey gasped as she struggled to extricate herself from the chair.

Julia, reaching her mother, gave in to full-blown sobbing. Hands covering her face, Julia's words sounded garbled.

Abbey stepped forward and enveloped her distraught daughter in her arms. "Hey, baby, what's the matter?"

She dropped her hands and spoke. "It's George," Julia wailed.

"What about George? Did something happen to him?"

"We broke up today." A fresh sob escaped. "He said he wanted to break up." Her shoulders shuddered. "With *meee*." The last part came out in an extended whine.

Abbey caught herself smiling and quickly turned her face away from Julia.

"Oh, please stop crying baby, I know it's hard for you to understand right now." Abbey hugged the girl again. "I know he's broken your heart."

After a few months of dating, and the conversations that she's had with Julia, Abbey really didn't care much for George but never made her feelings known.

It was something that happens to everyone when they ultimately fall in love. *Or have a deep crush.* Abbey wasn't willing to admit that Julia experienced real love for George.

After all, George rarely visited Julia at home and had never really introduced himself to her or Doug.

Abbey wanted to tell her daughter that she still had a lot to learn about love, but she wisely kept the words to herself, knowing Julia wasn't ready to hear it. She was grieving.

CHAPTER 1

Abbey held Julia in her arms. "Go ahead and cry, my baby. I know it hurts, but in the end, you'll recover." Then, a trite platitude escaped her before she could stop it. "I know it's hard for you to see, but it really wasn't meant to be." She cringed but continued. "I promise you'll find love again. You never know, maybe next time it will be right."

Julia never looked up, but the crying slowed. The phone in the house rang, interrupting their bonding. Abbey gave Julia one last hug and walked into the house to answer the phone.

"Hello?"

"What's wrong, Abbey?"

It was Doug, her husband. "Oh, nothing. Julia and I were out by the pool, talking."

"I thought Julia was going to the matinee with George?"

Abbey could hear the stress in his voice. He knew it wasn't "nothing."

"Well, apparently, they got into some sort of disagreement and George broke up with her."

Abbey listened to several seconds of silence.

"I see. I am going to get Chris and we will be home in about an hour… unless you need me sooner."

She heard the question in his words. "No, I think we should have some girls' time. We'll get this sorted out."

Doug barked a laugh. "It's going to take more than just a few hours to get that all ironed out."

"Yes, I know, but her poor heart is torn apart, and she needs me to help her mend it."

"You're a good mother, honey. Chris and I will stop by the sports store and get that helmet he's been asking for."

"Alright, when you get home, we can talk to Julia together."

"Sounds good," Doug said and disconnected.

CHAPTER 2

Doug

Doug pulled the car up to the *Boy Scouts of America* building and walked in. Waiting in the front entry was Chris.

The Scout leader, Mr. Bagley, waited for the rest of the Scouts to get in line.

"Alright, young men, turn to your parents and recite the Scouts' Oath."

Without hesitation, the group repeated the well-known oath of honor.

> *"On my honor, I will do my best*
> *to do my duty to God and my country*
> *and to obey the Scout Law;*
> *to help other people at all times;*
> *to keep myself physically strong,*
> *mentally awake, and morally straight."*

The Scout leader waited for them to finish and for them to again silence themselves. Then, they were released to their parents.

CHAPTER 2

Chris ran and jumped into Doug's arms. "Hey, Dad." He grinned from ear to ear.

"I have a surprise for you, Son. We're going to make a stop before we go home."

"Where? What is it?" Chris' words flew out of his mouth.

Doug laughed. "We're going and see about that helmet."

"Really?" Chris shouted.

He reminded Doug of a puppy, full of boundless energy and joy.

They turned to walk away when the Scout leader called them back.

Doug stepped over to the leader. "Good afternoon, Mr. Bagley."

"I just wanted to let you know how well Chris is doing in the Scouts. Over the last three months, he has really begun to work hard on his Oaths and drill lessons. He is the leader of the class. His model behavior is exceptional." He smiled at Chris. "So how old are you, Son?"

Chris smiled and looked at his dad. Doug smiled and looked at Bagley, "He will turn eleven later this year."

"That is terrific. With what Chris is doing, reciting all his oaths and being such a reliable Scout, I think he is ready to move on up to the next rank." Mr. Bagley raised an eyebrow. "I would even go so far to say that he is ready to be an Arrow of Light Scout."

Doug looked at Chris. "So, what do you think, Son? Are you ready to become an Arrow of Light Scout? There are some real responsibilities you have to take on to be the best of the best."

Chris' face lit up like a Christmas tree.

Doug glanced over at the Scout leader. They both smiled and looked back at Chris.

"I think that's a *yes*. Thank you." Doug extended his hand.

Mr. Bagley shook Doug's hand. "You have a real good son here." He turned and walked away.

Doug grabbed Chris' duffel bag and put his other arm around the boy. "How do you feel about being an Arrow of Light Scout?"

"I don't know, Dad. I really want to be a football player. I want to be a quarterback."

"Fair enough. Let's go and get that helmet, and then we can go and see what Mom and Julia think about you moving up the Scout ranks."

Doug and Chris walked into the house. Doug noticed Abbey and Julia in the kitchen fixing dinner just as Chris took off to his bedroom.

Abbey came over to greet Doug.

"Is she alright?" he asked.

"Yes, she'll be fine. Her little feelings were hurt."

"See? That is why I didn't want her around boys yet."

"Well, then, what *would you* have wanted?"

Doug squinted and hunched his shoulders, knowing his opinion was outrageous. "For her to wait till she was in college before she started having male friends?"

Abbey laughed. "That's not gonna happen. At least now we can monitor what they're doing, instead of guessing. Otherwise she could get talked into something really crazy." She hugged Doug, welcoming him home. "Trust me. At least she was at home when she got her heart broken. I'm just glad I was here to help break her fall. If she was in college and... remember what college she wants to go to?" She brushed Doug's cheek with her fingers. University of North Carolina. That is a far cry away from home. But today, she came home and we were able to talk face to face. She is doing much better... for now."

Doug tilted his head. "Yes. I get that for *now* she's better, but only until she goes back to school, and he starts wanting to talk again. See? That's what boys do. We want to see how much

CHAPTER 2

control we have over you ladies, so we act like we don't care. We make it seem like we are mad, but we are not. It's just a test."

"What are you talking about?" Abbey asked.

"I don't know," Doug said, shaking his head. They both laughed.

Julia walked in. "Hi, Dad," she said softly.

"Hey, my baby girl, how are you doing?"

"So, you heard." She shifted from foot to foot. "I'm ok-a-a-ay, I guess." She looked at her mother. "I'm tired. Gonna lay down for a while."

"Alright," Abbey said. She watched her until she disappeared from the room.

Doug followed Abbey into the kitchen, "So, Chris and I have some good news." He yelled for Chris.

It was only a few moments before Chris sprinted into the room.

"Son, tell your mom the good news," Doug said.

Chris' fair-skinned face blushed.

"Go on, tell Mommy what your Scout Leader said."

Chris just smiled.

Doug took over. "It's okay, I understand." He turned to his wife. "The Scout leader told us he thinks that our son is ready to become an Arrow of Light Scout."

"Oh my. That is amazing," Abbey said. She grabbed Chris and started tickling him. "So, you remembered your oaths?" she asked. Chris didn't answer, he just giggled. Abbey looked at Doug.

"Yes, he remembered everything. The leader said Chris was becoming a very good Scout." Doug looked back to Chris. "Now, remember what was said earlier. There are a lot of responsibilities when you become an Arrow of Light Scout."

"Like what?" Chris finally spoke.

Doug grabbed the paper the leader had given him and scanned it. "First, you have to demonstrate that you live by the principles of the Scout Oath and Law in your daily life."

WHOSE FAULT?

Abbey looked at Doug curiously. She waited to gain his attention.

Doug never looked up. "List the names of individuals who know you personally and would be willing to provide a recommendation on your behalf."

Abbey's eyes flew up, willing Doug to look at her.

Finally, Doug looked at her. Abbey was laughing. "What are you talking about? You know this little guy's first love is football."

"Yes, well, what's wrong with doing both of them? He can learn some discipline and some toughness."

Abbey raised her eyebrows skeptically.

"Look," Doug said, "I know what I am talking about and what this young fella needs. Just leave making this dude a man up to me and I will leave making my daughter a young lady up to you."

Abbey stared at Doug, waiting for more. "Are you sure you want to go there?"

Later Doug walked by Julia's bedroom door. He looked in. She was sitting on her bed with her pillow on her lap, looking out the window.

He knocked lightly and walked in. "Hey baby, what's going on?"

She sat silently, still staring out the window.

"Are you going to be all right?" he asked.

Julia nodded her head up and down.

"Then why aren't you talking?"

"I'm just thinking about what I did wrong for... him to act that way."

"What makes you think you did something wrong?"

A tear rolled down her face.

"Oh, my sweet girl." Doug sat next to her. "There is nothing wrong with you, I promise. You have just had your first dealing with love. I'm sure that your heart is heavy but don't ever think

CHAPTER 2

that you are at fault. It could have been anything. Sometimes it's just some little thing that makes another person act the way they do. You just continue being you and being the sweet young lady that you are."

Abbey arrived. She stood next to the door. She watched as Doug explained love to their daughter. And the more she watched Julia cry, the heavier her heart became.

"We'll just put this in God's hands," Doug said. He took her hand and began praying. "God, you care deeply for broken-hearted people. This is a promise You make to those You are close to. We pray for all those who are crippled by broken relationships. Our hearts take the blow of disappointment. We feel crushed because our hopes are dashed. If pieces of our hearts have been lost, or are held captive by another, Lord, please recover them and bring them back to us and miraculously put us back together so that our hearts are whole again. You are the Mender of broken hearts. We ask for this miracle in the name of Jesus." Doug hugged Julia, then stood up and saw Abbey watching. In a silent exchange, Abbey walked in and Doug went out.

A few minutes later, Abbey walked into their bedroom. "Thank you," she said.

Doug glanced over. "It wasn't the time to go in there all strong and tough." He sighed. "Her tender heart is torn apart, and I just thought I should go in there just being her dad."

"Sometimes you are the gentlest man I know," Abbey said. She leaned over and gave Doug a kiss on the cheek.

Chris walked into the room. "What's the matter with Julia? She won't talk to me."

Doug grabbed Chris and tackled him. "Where are your helmet and jersey? You are out of uniform, kid!"

Chris forgot all about Julia and ran to his room for his equipment.

"Hey, Doug. I want to discuss something with you." She paused a moment. "What do you think of letting the kids go to their auntie's house? It's been a long summer and I think it would be good for them to get away for a while." Abbey's face showed concern. "Especially with her bruised heart, now would be a great time for Julia to get away so she can… get herself back together."

Doug didn't answer. He just turned away.

"Really, Doug, what do you think about this idea?"

"How are they going to get out there?"

"We have enough money to buy them airline tickets. They can fly and Beth will get them when they get off the airplane."

"Fly all by themselves? Are you sure?" Doug questioned. "I don't know about that."

Abbey sighed and moved to face Doug. "It's a very short flight and right now, not only can they use the time away, but we can use this for some 'us' time together. Also, a flight attendant will watch over them and escort them from the plane."

"Well, we'll be going to church tomorrow," Doug said. "And we'll just pray that we do the right thing. But I do want to talk about this some more before we make a decision."

Pastor Andrews finished his sermon and walked to the front door of the church. He waited as people passed by, congratulated him on the sermon and spoke briefly to each other.

Abbey walked up to Pastor Andrews with Julia and Chris. Both wore big smiles.

"What are the smiles for? My sermon was that good?" Pastor Andrews asked.

CHAPTER 2

"Well, Pastor, Julia and Chris will be spending the rest of the summer with my sister in Chicago." The kids walked away. "This will be a great time for Deacon Campbell and me to have some quality time together. Just as you suggested in our last counseling session."

"Yes, yes, a very deserving time indeed," Pastor Andrews said as he extended his hand to another couple passing by.

"So, what does Mr. Campbell think about this? I know he is so guarded with those children."

"He really wasn't sure that they should be going all by themselves, but I explained to him that we were going to the airport and make sure they were boarded on the airplane and when they arrived, my sister would be at the gate waiting for them."

"Did he agree to that?"

"Well, I had to persuade him just a little, trying to make him see it my way, but in the end, I think he understood."

"Alright, Sister Campbell, I hope everything works out for the best."

"I'm sure it will," Abbey said then turned and walked away to talk to others.

Pastor Andrews turned away and came face-to-face with Deacon Campbell.

"Nice sermon, Pastor," Doug Campbell said.

"Thank you, sir. I just left your wife. She's standing… there, over by the choir seats. We were talking about the kids. I guess you all are sending them to Chicago?"

"We have talked about it," Doug said, "but I am pretty much still up in the air on that."

"Oh. I must have misunderstood. I thought it was all arranged." Pastor Andrews rubbed his chin in thought. "Although, the statistics suggest that air travel is safer than any other way of travel."

"Yes, I understand that, but I am not sure I am ready for them to travel alone."

"I'm sure you and Abbey will make the right decision." Pastor Andrews smiled, extended his hand, and walked away to talk to another couple.

Abbey and the kids were walking out of the church when Doug caught up with them.

"Are you attending afternoon service?" Abbey asked him.

"I was thinking about it; I will let you know in a couple of hours, my back is starting to bother me." He stretched his shoulders and back.

"I heard you and the Pastor were talking about the kids."

Abbey nodded. "Yeah, I was telling him that finally we were going to have some quality time together. With the kids gone, I might get to see what New Orleans really looks like."

"Abbey, we were going to talk more about the kids and this trip. I haven't had time to think about it. Or pray about it."

"Hey, I just brought it up and he asked questions. I never said the plans were finalized."

"Well, okay then. But I'm still not sure how comfortable I am sending the kids off on an airplane without one of us with them. Safe or not, I'm not convinced this is what we should be doing."

"All right. So, do you have time to fly with them?" Abbey asked.

Doug sighed. "I know I would have to go through all kinds of red tape trying to get the time off from my job."

"I checked with the airlines. They said as long as Julia is older than thirteen, she may fly unaccompanied, and that Chris could fly with her."

"I guess that simplifies things for you," Doug said.

Abbey narrowed her eyes. "That's a bit rude."

CHAPTER 2

"They're only kids." Doug threw his hands up. A low growl showed his frustration. "What if your sister is late getting to the airport? There are so many things that could go wrong."

Abbey tilted her head.

"What?" Doug asked.

"We always see things differently," Abbey said. "If there was a cup on the table with water filled halfway, you would say it's half-empty and I would say it's half-full. We are never on the same page."

"So which page are you on when it comes to our kids?" Doug asked. "Are you willing to take unnecessary risks?"

Abbey walked out the side door of the church and slammed it behind her.

She walked to the car, got into the driver's side, and waited for Doug and the kids to get there. After Doug closed the car door, Abbey looked into the back seat and waited as Julia helped Chris with his seat belt.

Doug planned to start a conversation but thought better of it as Abbey was driving and not really talking with anyone. Her body language showed tension. After pulling in the driveway, Abbey turned the car off and got out. Everyone else sat there and watched her unlock the door to the house then walk in without looking back.

Doug helped the kids get out and waited a few minutes to recollect his thoughts. He took a few deep breaths and then walked into the house. He found Abbey in the living room, drinking a glass of water.

"Look, I don't want to argue about this. I understand you want some time together, but we still have to think about the well-being of our kids. I couldn't have a good time if I thought the kids were in harm's way or not safe."

WHOSE FAULT?

Abbey stared blankly out the window, her hand over her mouth. Slowly, she took her hand away from her quivering lips. "If I thought the kids were going to be hurt in any way, there's no way I would even suggest for them to go. But personally, I don't think there is anything to worry about. Julia is very responsible and will do exactly what we ask her to do."

"Alright then, for the sake of argument, let's say they did fly, and your sister didn't show up, for whatever reason. If they called you, what would you do?" Doug asked.

Abbey stepped away from the window and stopped in front of him. "I would tell them to wait for her and not leave the airport. As a matter of fact, I would even go as far as to tell them to go back inside the terminal and wait for her inside."

"That's putting a lot on a seventeen-year-old kid," Doug said. "Especially while she is toting around an even younger kid. What if it takes a while and the kids get hungry? I mean, there is just so much that can happen in just a little time."

Abbey sighed. "I believe my sister is responsible enough to know what is important. I don't think she will abandon my kids at an airport."

Doug nodded in agreement and sat on the couch.

After a few moments, Abbey walked out of the room and into the kitchen. She yelled, "Are you hungry?"

Doug yelled back, "Yes." He'd gone to their bedroom. He threw off his shoes and relaxed, he yawned and stretched… and eventually fell asleep.

The bed rocked and Doug blinked several times then slowly turned over to see what was happening.

Abbey was sitting at the bottom of the bed, looking at him.

CHAPTER 2

"What time is it?" he asked.

"Eight o'clock in the evening," Abbey said, looking serious.

"How long have I been asleep?" He tried to look at the alarm clock, but Abbey was blocking it.

"Long enough for the food you asked for to grow cold."

Doug sat up and rubbed the back of his neck. He cocked his head, listening. "Where are the kids?"

"They are in their rooms; it's almost their bedtime."

Doug looked at her, dazed.

"School tomorrow, today is Sunday, remember?"

"Funny!" Doug said. He stood up and moved toward the bathroom.

When he came out, Abbey was still sitting on the bed.

"Is there something wrong?" he asked.

"Your dinner is on the table," Abbey said and left.

Doug stared at her until she disappeared out of sight. On his way to the kitchen, he stopped by Chris' room. "So how did you enjoy church today?"

"It was okay, Daddy."

"Is there anything you heard the pastor say that you need me to explain?"

"No, Daddy."

"Alright then, on your knees, we need to say our prayers before we go to sleep." Doug held Chris' hand as he recited the Lord's Prayer.

"Our Father, which art in heaven, Hallowed be thy Name. Thy kingdom come. Thy will be done on earth, as it is in heaven. Give us this day our daily bread. And forgive us our trespasses, as we forgive them that trespass against us. And lead us not into temptation,

But deliver us from evil. For Thine is the kingdom, the power, and the glory, for ever and ever. Amen."

WHOSE FAULT?

Chris jumped up quickly and jumped into the bed. Doug stayed down and prayed for a few more seconds.

When he stood, Chris asked, "Daddy, what were you praying about?"

"I was asking God to look over you as you sleep and to keep you safe."

Doug grabbed the end of the covers and pulled them over Chris, then gently kissed him on the forehead. "Good night, Son."

Slowly he walked to the door, turned the light off, and closed the door.

"Hello baby," he said as he entered Julia's room. Julia quickly pulled the covers over her body. "Dad!" she cried, embarrassed.

Doug laughed, "Young lady, I used to change your diapers. Besides, I just came here to say goodnight to you before your mother gets upset. You were supposed to be in your bed and under the covers twenty minutes ago. And you know how your mom gets when it comes to school nights."

"Yeah, I know Dad, I was just finishing up this last paragraph."

"Did you say your prayers?"

"Yes, I did. I never get into bed without saying them."

"Alright." Doug kissed her on the forehead and started to walk away. "Hey, tomorrow you and I are going to have a talk."

"A talk about what?" Julia squeaked.

"Don't fret about it, but when I get home from work, we'll talk. Good night."

Doug walked into the kitchen where Abbey was sitting down.

"There is your supper," she said, pointing to the other side of the table. "It's gone cold again. Where were you?"

"I was kissing the kids goodnight."

"Did you talk to Julia about the flight?"

"No, I didn't. I still haven't finished talking to you about it," Doug said. "But I did tell her we would talk tomorrow."

CHAPTER 2

"Are you going to talk to her about it then?"

"Probably, depending on where we are after finishing up our conversation."

Abbey hesitated, then put both her elbows on the table and rested her head in the palms of her hands. From behind her hands, she asked, "So what is the problem?" She removed her hands and looked at him. "Do you even want to spend time with me?"

Doug stood up, walked around, and sat in the chair next to her.

"Of course. You know I want to spend time with you, that's all we have been talking about for the last six months. I just want to make sure the kids are safe. Once I know they are safe, I can enjoy you and wherever we go."

"I tell you what," Doug said, "why don't we just take them down to your sister's house? Then we can go somewhere from there."

"How is a few extra days spent with the kids going to hurt?"

Abbey sat silently, waiting until she figured out what she wanted to say.

"I'll have to check with my boss and see if she would allow me to take a couple of extra days. But she won't be in until Wednesday."

"Alright," Doug said. "Until then." He walked back to the other side of the table and sat down.

"Would you like me to warm your food up?" Abbey asked.

Doug looked down at the plate, "Yes, I would, thank you."

CHAPTER 3

Doug

The next day Doug walked into the house exhausted. He slammed his keys down on the counter and walked into the bedroom.

Abbey's head appeared through the doorway to their bathroom. "Are you okay?"

"Yes, just frustrated with that job. I can't begin to tell you what I just went through. Now more than ever, I know that I need a break away from there."

"Well, I don't mean to be a bearer of bad news, but instead of waiting on Wednesday, I called Cheryl today. She said she could not afford to let me go more than the days she has already allotted me."

Doug exhaled, sat on the bed, and looked at Abbey.

"Well, why don't you rest a bit before you go in and talk to Julia?" Abbey asked.

"That is a good idea—right now isn't a good time anyway."

"Dinner will be ready in about half an hour. Are you hungry?"

CHAPTER 3

"I'm more tired and upset than hungry, but I know when I finally wind down, I will be ready to eat something."

"How about a hot bath? That will relax you."

Abbey went into the bathroom and turned on the water. "I checked on the airline tickets today and if we book them early, they will be cheap."

Doug never answered, just laid back and waited for the tub to fill up.

"Did you hear me?" Abbey asked as she grabbed a face and bath towel from the closet.

"Yes, I heard you," Doug said as he slowly rolled out of bed and walked into the bathroom.

Abbey startled when she heard Doug yell.

"Yow!"

She hurried into the bathroom. Doug was standing near the bathtub.

'That water is hot!"

"I'm sorry Hon, but I did add some cold water."

"Not enough." Doug moaned about being fricasseed as he turned on the cold water. He watched as Abbey walked out of the bathroom.

Abbey stopped just short of the bedroom door and tippy-toed back towards the bathroom.

Doug tested the water again with his toes. He stuck his foot in the water and quickly withdrew his leg. "Wow!"

He sat on the side of the tub and waited for the cold water to cool the tub down, thinking of what to say to Julia.

Abbey walked away, smiling.

"I heard you," Doug said.

"You heard me smile?" Abbey laughed and walked out of the bedroom.

WHOSE FAULT?

Doug walked into the family room where the ladies were watching television.

"Your dinner is in there on the table," Abbey said without looking at him.

Doug walked into the kitchen. He looked around for a few minutes and then back to the family room.

"Where is Chris?" he asked, looking around.

"Is there something wrong?" Abbey asked.

"I need to talk to the three of you. Is it alright to turn the TV off?"

Julia walked over and turned the TV off, then yelled for Chris.

Doug sat down between the kids and waited for Abbey to return from the kitchen.

"What do you two think of flying to your auntie's house next weekend?" he asked.

"We already knew we were going over to Auntie's house," Chris said.

"Yes, but did you know you would be flying?"

"No." Julia looked at her mom. "Are you going with us?"

"No, I have to work." Julia looked over to Doug. "Your auntie will be waiting at the gate when you get off the airplane," Doug explained.

"So, we're flying alone?" Julia asked.

Abbey walked over and sat down beside Julia. "Auntie Beth will be standing there as you get off the plane. It's just a quick flight there."

Chris sat silently and let Julia do all the talking.

"Are you okay with this?" Doug asked.

"I don't know... I have never flown all by myself."

"You won't be alone, you will be with Chris," Doug said.

Chris sat up and looked at Julia.

CHAPTER 3

"If you don't want to fly alone, we understand," Doug said. He glanced at Abbey. "We just thought you would like to go there instead of spending the last few weeks of your summer vacation hanging around the house."

Julia sat still, staring at the blank television screen.

"Well, think about it, we'll give you a chance to think about it. If this is something you don't want to do or something you're uncomfortable with… we will understand."

Doug stood up and walked back to the table to eat.

Chris grabbed the remote and turned the TV back on. Abbey sat with Julia and watched TV until time for bed.

"Alright you two, it's getting close to bedtime," Abbey said.

Julia waited as Chris went to his room. "Mom, can I talk to you?"

Abbey leaned forward. "Is something wrong?"

"I was just thinking about what Dad was saying." She fidgeted with her hands for a moment. "I have always been afraid of flying and only felt comfortable because you or Dad were there. I don't know if I am going to like flying without one of you there."

"We understand baby, we just thought we would ask."

Julia grabbed Abbey's arm. "Mom, I don't want Daddy to think I'm scared or just don't want to go with Chris."

"Your dad would never think like that, sweetie. We just thought it would be nice for you two to go and we would try to take a few days and go somewhere by ourselves."

Julia lowered her head.

"What's the matter?" Abbey asked as she moved closer to Julia.

"Oh, nothing. I'll go, Mom."

"What's the matter, baby?" Abbey asked again, worry showing on her face.

"Julia, we don't want you to go if you really don't want to. That's not what this is about. It's completely up to you."

WHOSE FAULT?

"I'm alright, Mom." Julia gave her a hug and walked out of the room.

The next day, Doug arrived home earlier than usual. He walked into the bedroom and surprised Abbey. "What are you doing home so early?" she asked.

"I've had enough with that place. I'm still upset from yesterday's shenanigans. So, I told the boss that I needed to go home."

Chris ran into the room and jumped on the bed. Doug grabbed him and tackled him. Chris yelled, "Touchdown."

Doug laughed and said, "No, I tackled you on the one-yard line."

Chris sat up and hugged Doug.

Doug looked up and smiled at him.

"What?" Doug asked.

"Dad, can you get me a Bears football jersey before I go to Auntie's house?"

"What do you want a Bears jersey for? We live in New Orleans. You should want a Saints jersey."

"Nope, I want a Bears jersey."

Abbey walked out of the room.

"Alright, buddy, but my team will do better than yours." Doug laughed.

Chris jumped out of bed and ran into the hallway, then suddenly he appeared and jumped on the bed again. "Touchdown, Dad." He grinned.

"The ref threw a flag for off-sides," Doug said, laughing.

Chris furrowed his eyebrows. "What does that mean?"

"That means you did something that you were not supposed to do."

"Like what?"

Doug, looking surprised at the sudden questions, was trying to come up with an answer when Julia walked in.

CHAPTER 3

"You can be my cheerleader," Chris said.

"No, not today, Chris. Dad, can we talk?"

"Of course, baby," Doug said.

"It's halftime," he said to Chris. "Go see what your mom is doing."

When he'd gone, Doug turned to Julia. "Is everything okay?"

"I wanted to tell you… well, I'm sorry for how I acted before. About the trip. I know you and mom need some time together."

Doug just listened as Julia finished her thoughts.

"Baby, your mom and I can always find time to be together. We just thought this was a good time for you and your brother to spend some time with family. Yes, we were going to plan something while you two were away. But that's not the only reason we wanted you to go."

"Well, I just came in here to tell you I've decided I will go. And I will take care of Chris while we are there."

Doug waited for Julia to say something else.

Silence.

"So, what's going on with you and George, or is it not alright for me to ask that question?"

"It's okay, Dad. He called me a couple of times but… it's not the same as before."

"So, getting away may help a little, don't you think?"

"It could. But I'm going to leave my phone here so that I don't have to talk to him."

"Hey, at least it didn't take long for you to get back on your feet."

Julia smiled then stared at the floor.

Doug broke the silence. "Well, your brother is kind of happy. He even asked for a Bears jersey."

Julia stood up. "Dad, Chris has been asking for a Bears jersey almost every day since he got the helmet."

"So… is there something you want to take with you?" Doug asked.

"No, just going to take my backpack with my books and begin freshening up and get ready for twelfth grade."

"You don't need to worry about getting ready. You, my dear, are already ready. Every class last year you scored an A, remember?"

"Maybe a better backpack would be nice. I heard they have them at the student store with our school mascot and name on them."

My baby is in the twelfth grade, my, how time flies.

Julia left the bedroom as Abbey and Chris came in.

"Hey, Mom, Chris," Julia said.

Doug looked at his wife. "Alright, honey. Go ahead and purchase the airline tickets, but please make sure that your sister will be there to receive our babies."

CHAPTER 4

Julia and Chris

Abbey was in Chris' room when Julia walked in. "Are you finished packing?" Abbey asked.

"Yes just a few more things. I don't think I'm going to need a lot of clothes, I don't know anyone except Auntie Beth, so I won't be going anywhere.

Julia reached for Chris' helmet. "Did you remember to put his jersey in there?"

Julia rolled her eyes. "I still don't believe he is going to take a helmet on the airplane with him."

"Well, it was either the helmet or the football. I can see him trying to play catch with the pilot." They both laughed.

Doug walked into the room with Chris right behind him.

"What's so funny?" he asked.

Chris took his helmet from Julia and the two ladies started laughing again.

"Are you finished packing? The flight leaves in three hours," Doug said.

"Yes. Mom just checked on that," Julia answered.

"We're thorough, at least. Now, you two go into the kitchen and fix yourselves a sandwich. I don't want you getting hungry at the airport. It's much too expensive to buy a meal there."

As soon as the kids left the room, Doug turned to Abbey. "Are you sure you want to be without the kids?" He smiled.

"This is your last chance. No turning back once they're inside the airport."

"This is a much-needed break, Doug. You know that. It gives you and me some time to relax and reconnect."

Doug locked the front door, then headed to the car.

"We got everything, right?" He started the car.

Abbey walked away from the counter and approached Doug and the kids. *That was a nice young lady. So helpful.*

"Okay, everybody, the flight number is 1015 and it departs out of gate 5 at 4:30. They'll start boarding about 4:00."

"I'm hungry," Chris said. He was looking at a McDonald's across the hall.

"I told you to eat something," Doug said.

"Oh Doug, go get that young man something to eat, it's not like this happens all the time," Abbey said.

"It may not happen all the time, but we're not usually at the airport."

Julia held out her hand. "Dad, I'll take him."

Doug gave her a twenty-dollar bill and sat down on a chair.

As soon as they walked away, Abbey turned to Doug. "My, how our daughter has matured. She doesn't even talk about that boy at all."

Julia returned with two dollars and twenty-six cents.

Doug laughed. "Where is the rest of my change?

CHAPTER 4

Julia pointed to the bag. "In here. I figured since you had already given in to Chris getting something to eat, it really didn't matter if I got myself something too."

Doug laughed and turned to Abbey. "I'm getting conned by my own children."

A few minutes later, a lady's voice sounded over the loudspeakers. "We are ready to begin boarding for flight 1015 to Chicago. Please have your boarding pass ready."

Doug handed Julia the two tickets and gave her a kiss on the cheek then a hug. "Two weeks will go fast. And try to have fun."

Abbey and Doug switched, saying goodbye to each of their children. Doug grabbed Chris and squeezed him. "When you get home, it's going to be the Saints against the Bears." He reached into his pocket and brought out two tickets. Showing them to Chris, he said. "See? You and I are going to the game."

Chris grabbed Doug around the waist and waited for him to kneel down and then gave him a kiss on the cheek. "See you later, Dad." Chris waved at the woman at the gate. "Look, me and my dad is going to the football game."

She smiled politely.

The kids started walking toward the door when Doug noticed Chris's helmet, still in the chair.

"Hey, do you want this?"

Chris ran back, grabbed the helmet, and ran back to Julia. They both waved goodbye as they entered the jet's boarding bridge.

Abbey moved around to peer down the skybridge so she could take one last look at them before they entered the airplane.

Julia gave one last wave and disappeared into the huge jet.

A puddle of water started gathering in Abbey eyes. She reached into her purse and grabbed some tissue.

"Are you crying?" Doug asked.

Abbey turned away from him and finished drying her tears.

Both of them walked towards the large window. As they watched, the jet pulled away from the jet bridge and began its departure, slowly heading to the runway.

Doug turned and began walking away. Abbey stayed at the window and waited for the only airplane on the runway to take off.

CHAPTER 5

Abbey and Doug

Doug took Abbey's hand. "Alright, let's go. We have dinner plans in a couple of hours."

Abbey looked at Doug and smiled. "Oh? And when did you make these plans?"

"I'm taking my wife to the most exquisite restaurant in New Orleans. I am going to spoil you for the next two weeks," Doug said. He wrapped an arm around her shoulders and turned them to leave.

"I think I'm going to like this, and you spoiling me is something I haven't had since we were courting."

Doug looked at Abbey and they both laughed. "Are you thinking what I am thinking?"

Abbey let out a loud but quick laugh. Thinking of how they met, she said, "You fell over that stump hard." She laughed.

"I didn't fall all that hard." Doug grinned.

"You tried to play it all off, which you did a horrible job of." Abbey laughed. "When my friends laughed, I knew that I had to go and help you up."

"I thought my landing was great. I might have scored a ten." Doug smiled. "But I did land you in the process."

"But the first date was horrible," Doug recounted the memory. "I wanted so badly to take you somewhere special, but the way that my bank account was... *ahem*, set up..." The rest of his sentence faded away. No need to finish—they both remembered how penniless he was. They broke into laughter.

Doug smirked. "Well, this time, I have some money." Then, each remembered where they'd gone on their first date.

Both of them stopped walking at the same time. They turned to face each other. "The golden arches." Their faces reflected joy from the memory.

They walked out of the airport to the car. "Come on, let's go see what New Orleans is really about." Doug smiled.

Doug grabbed Abbey's hand. "How about a margarita? It's still too early to go to the restaurant," he said. "Besides, I have hotel reservations nearby."

Abbey smiled. "This is going to fun. Beignets and coffee for breakfast?"

"Café Du Monde? You know it."

After a nice conversation and cocktails, they arrived at the hotel, checked in and had the bellman take their bags to the room.

"Let's take a stroll through the French Quarters," Doug said.

"Wait, let me grab my sweater," Abbey said as she stopped the bellman and grabbed her garment.

"We need to do more things like this," Doug said as he took her hand and guided her across the street.

"It sure feels good out here... a little breezy," Abbey said. "Nice. Not too hot and not too cold."

"The perfect time to take a walk." Doug smiled, leaned over and gave Abbey a peck on the lips. He stopped in front of a restaurant and waited for Abbey, who was sightseeing.

CHAPTER 5

"What are you waiting for?" Abbey asked.

"We're here." Doug smiled. "We have dinner reservations... here." He pointed to the door, opened it, and waited for Abbey to walk through.

"Ooohhh. This is a nice place... how did you find it?"

"Just got lucky, I guess. There were plenty to choose from, but I wanted the one with the best food and ambiance."

The waiter stood next to Doug and waited for his attention. "We have you located in the center of the floor, or would you like another seat?"

"No, that table is perfect," Doug said. "It's the one I saw on your brochure. The one near the water fountain."

After about an hour of eating and reminiscing, Doug turned to Abbey. "Well, I guess we could head on back to the hotel. I'm getting a little tired."

They stopped at the crosswalk across the street from the hotel, stunned by what they saw.

"What's going on in the lobby?" Doug asked.

"I don't know. I hope we can get to the elevator," Abbey answered.

Doug walked in first and held Abbey's hand as he navigated through the crowd.

A bunch of people gathered, all staring at the television on the wall.

Doug bumped into one of the men standing. The man moved over a step and exposed the TV screen.

Doug glanced at the screen and then back at the gentleman. "So, what's going on here?"

The man looked at Doug. The news announcer started talking. The man turned his gaze back to the TV.

"Has something happened?" Doug tried again to get information.

"Come on, baby," Abbey nudged him. "Let's go up to the room."

Doug turned to leave.

Just then, the man spoke in a hushed voice. "An airplane crashed. It's bad."

Abbey had taken a couple of steps towards the elevator but felt Doug let go of her hand.

"What's the matter, hon? Abbey asked.

Doug shouldered his way closer to the television, elbowing people out the way. He yelled, "What flight was it?"

No one responded. They were all mesmerized watching the newscast.

He yelled louder. "What flight crashed?"

Abbey heard Doug yell and walked faster to catch up with him. "What's the matter?" she yelled, trying to get his attention among the crowd's noise. Doug kept moving closer to the television.

When he arrived at the screen, he stopped and fixed his gaze on the bottom of the screen. The channel was scrolling a band at the bottom giving the flight information. He finally was close enough to hear.

"Again, breaking news," the anchor said. "A domestic flight has crashed. We do not know the extent of fatalities at this point. Firefighters are diligently working to put out the fire. Then, they can begin to search the rubble for survivors."

Abbey wound through the people and finally caught up with him. "What's the matter? She tapped him on the shoulder.

Doug stared into the screen, waiting for the airline name and flight number.

The man anchoring the news began to speak again.

CHAPTER 5

"To recap, this afternoon there was a domestic airplane crash, Flight 1015 crashed shortly after leaving Louis Armstrong New Orleans International Airport. According to witnesses, there was a loud explosion and witnesses on the ground noticed flames coming out of the number two engine. The large 737 Boeing jet began to lose altitude. Sadly, it crashed just shortly after takeoff. We have a reporter on scene now."

The TV screen showed a video of flames rising from the wreckage. Firefighters had launched several hoses, spewing massive amounts of water at the base of the fire. "This is Chad Banks, on scene, a few miles north of the airport. You're seeing live footage of the crash." He touched his finger to his ear. "We have just been informed by authorities that the odds are against anyone surviving. The jet had full tanks of fuel, which exploded as it hit the ground. The airplane had just taken off and was headed for Chicago. The names of the victims are being held pending notification of family and the NTSB investigation. There seems to be no terrorist activity involved in the crash. Please stay tuned for more information. Film updates at eleven. Chad Banks, at the scene of the crash of Flight 1015."

Doug stood in front of the television, motionless. With a shocked and disbelief look on his face. He stared into the screen, slowly shaking his head from side to side. "No...no, no," he whispered.

Abbey's face began to register signs of seriousness as she slowly comprehended what was going on. She stood behind Doug with her hand covering her mouth, silently losing her strength. Doug turned slowly to find Abbey, directly behind him, gasping for air. She was panting very heavily as Doug grabbed her upper arm and walked her over to a nearby seat.

"What's wrong?" A lady asked. "I'm a licensed nurse."

WHOSE FAULT?

Abbey reached for her hand and tried to speak but couldn't get out any words.

"Sir! Do you have any idea what is wrong with your wife?" The nurse asked again.

All Doug could mutter was, "Flight 1015."

"What about 1015?" The nurse asked

Abbey began reaching for the nurse again, still trying to talk with her.

"Do anyone in here know these folks?" the nurse yelled.

Doug sat beside Abbey and held her. With a solemn, quiet voice, he spoke. "Abbey, our children were on that flight."

Abbey broke out in sobs. Her shoulders jerked as she wept for her children. She inhaled a ragged breath, folded her arms around her body and rocked back and forth. She refused to be consoled by Doug's comfort. Her darlings were gone.

"We have to make it home," Doug told Abbey. "They have to have a way to contact us." He tugged at Abbey, but she refused to stand up.

She looked up at Doug with tears pouring from her eyes. She shook her head, *no*.

Doug said, "But we have to go home."

"Wait! Wait," the nurse said, "I will get someone to take you home. You are in no condition to be driving."

"No. We'll... get home." His words came out haltingly. "I'll take... care of it." Doug stood up and grabbed Abbey's hand. She resisted.

"If I leave here..." She lowered her head and spoke softly. "It's... *real*." Another wave of sobbing began. She put her head in her hands and let the wracking anguish overtake her.

After a bit, Doug gently touched her arm. This time, she stood up.

CHAPTER 5

Doug looked around, assessing the crowd. He noticed that everyone in the hotel was reacting in their own way. Doug pulled Abbey through the door. The nurse followed.

The hotel manager had followed them. He asked, "Is there anything we can do?"

Doug didn't turn around to answer. He was in automatic mode, moving only by instinct, feeling an urgent need to protect his wife and get home. They walked to their car; he waited for Abbey to sit down then slowly closed the door. Turning his head, he saw the crowd in the hotel, talking and pointing at them, apparently observing their misery through the windows.

"Here is my number." The nurse handed Doug her business card. "If there is anything I can do to help or even console the both of you, just give me a call."

The hotel manager waited for the nurse to walk away and approached the car. "I'm so sorry for your loss. "I'll take care of your reservations. Refund your deposit. Is there anything I can do to help you? Send a catered meal to your home?"

Doug didn't register the comments. He started the car. The radio was playing a special announcement. Quickly, he reached over and turned the radio off. Abbey leaned over, resting her head on the window. She stared silently through the windshield. On the ride, the only thing making noise was the engine. After a long and very quiet trip back home, Doug slowly turned down the street toward home.

He pulled into the driveway very slowly, got out, and opened the passenger door. Abbey startled when he opened the door. He reached for her arm and guided her out of the car.

They walked to the house slowly as Abbey pressed her face into his shoulder. As they approached the house, they heard the phone ringing. A neighbor watering her grass whispered, "It's been ringing a lot."

WHOSE FAULT?

Doug turned slowly and acknowledged her and inserted his key into the door. He closed the door and looked out the window. *It's going to be a long time getting over this one,* he thought as he watched the neighbors and friends gather outside.

He let the curtain close, and the phone started ringing again. Doug walked towards the phone as Abbey went to the couch. She sat down as Doug picked up the receiver.

Carefully, Doug listened while looking over to Abbey. Tears silently fell from his eyes.

"What are they saying?" Abbey asked.

Doug just looked at her but remained on the phone. After a few minutes, he slowly hung up the phone and sat down next to Abbey.

"So, what did they say?" Abbey asked again.

Doug spoke as if each word tortured to his body. "They were... just letting us know." A long pause came. Doug cleared his throat and swiped at his eyes. "Uh, that... in fact there was an accident... and that Flight 1015... uh..." He paused for a minute to gather his strength and to again clear his throat. Then, his words came out all in a rush. "That Flight 1015 crashed shortly after takeoff." Another lengthy silence. "He was giving me all of this legal mumbo jumbo." Doug waved his hand through the air. "You know...covering his ass."

"Didn't he say anything about the kids?" Abbey asked desperately.

Doug sighed and hung his head. "No... he didn't say anything about any... survivors. He did say that there is an investigation going forward and that..." He took a deep but shuddering breath. "That all facts will be released from the NTSB."

Abbey reached over and grabbed an empty water glass on the table. Chris had drunk from it before leaving for the airport. She held the glass to her heart.

CHAPTER 5

"I want to go to the airport," Doug said. "I want more answers." He grabbed the keys and walked to the door, held it open, and turned to Abbey.

"Are you coming?"

Abbey sat quietly staring into Chris' glass.

"Abbey?" Doug asked again. He waited for a few seconds and slowly let the door close.

Before the door shut completely, Abbey grabbed the knob and walked out.

Abbey hurried next to Doug. "So, what are you going to ask them? What are you going to say? What are you going to do?" She fired the questions at him.

"I don't know what I am going to do right now. I just know at the airport is where I am supposed to be right now."

Just as he put the car in reverse to leave the driveway, Pastor Andrews pulled up. Doug put the car into park, shut the engine off, and got out. Abbey waited in the car.

"I just heard the news," Pastor Andrews said sadly. "One of the ushers at the church just told me what happened. Was it the flight with Julia and Chris on it?"

Doug nodded.

"You must pray on it," Pastor Andrews said. "You must pray."

Doug stared at Pastor Andrews without speaking.

Pastor Andrews sighed and shook his head. "I don't have the *reason why*, Doug. I'm so sorry." Tears began to fall from both men's faces. "I wish I could tell you why, but God only knows why this happened."

Doug just stood, absorbing the pastor's words. Abbey walked up.

"Hello, Abbey," Pastor Andrews said. He moved forward to offer her a hug.

WHOSE FAULT?

She pulled away. "Why my two children? We have prayed and have lived our lives following Christ. Why were our kids taken?" she asked, her voice belligerent.

"Pray and the answers will come," Pastor Andrews said. "God doesn't make mistakes, ask and you shall receive your answer."

Abbey walked closer to the pastor. "There isn't an answer in this world that is going to be good enough for me." Her eyebrows furrowed, her eyes still red from crying. Now she was angry. "My kids went to church every Sunday; they said their prayers every night before they went to sleep. Why are they gone?" Abbey asked. "Why are they gone?" she repeated, louder and angrier this time. Fresh tears rolled down her cheeks.

Pastor Andrews offered his handkerchief to Abbey, but she refused.

"My kids loved God, they *wanted* to go to church. We didn't have to force them, *ever*. What could they have done or what could we have done for God to punish us and take them away?"

"Sometimes life is so unfair," Pastor Andrews said. "And I know that, without the answers, the pain seems excruciating. But remember, God will never put more on you than you can handle. And He isn't punishing any of you. Whatever the reasons are, we just have to pray and try to understand."

"I don't understand and I don't *want* to understand." Abbey's voice rose, becoming louder.

Doug put his arms around her; she broke free and ran back into the house.

Doug watched her until she closed the door and then turned back to Pastor Andrews. "I hope this is not a test of my faith," he said and walked towards the house.

Pastor Andrews, sensing their pain, returned to his car and drove away.

CHAPTER 5

Doug walked into the house looking for Abbey. He found her lying across the bed.

"Come on, baby, we need to make it down to the airport."

"Why?" she said quietly. "They are not there!"

Doug silently agreed with her. "I know they are not there, but I believe their souls are. They may need us."

"What are you talking about?" Abbey screamed.

"Don't you get it? Our kids are dead!"

She didn't answer. She was crying too hard to speak.

"Well, I'm going. I don't know what I'll see… I don't know what they are going to say, I don't know why but I am still going." Doug walked away and went out the door.

Abbey rushed out the door a few moments later. "I'm sorry. I didn't mean to scream at you."

"I understand," Doug said. "Maybe I need to go there so that I can scream at someone. I don't know why, but I'm going. I know they are not there, but I'm going. I don't have any answers, but I'm going.

It was close to midnight when they arrived at the airport. News media were still there, wandering around trying to get a scoop.

Doug approached a woman at the ticket counter.

"Is there something I can help you with?" she asked cautiously.

Doug knew she'd registered their lack of luggage and seen the horror-stricken looks on their faces. Doug took a breath. *Say it out loud. It's real. Nothing will fix it.* "Our children were on Flight 1015.

The woman threw a hand over her mouth. She picked up a phone and punched some numbers. After a second, she said, "At the check-in. I've got family."

A few minutes later, a man in a suit walked over to the counter. The woman walked a few steps back with him. They spoke in hushed tones, then returned. The man came out from behind the counter, offered his hand to Doug. After they shook hands, he asked them to follow him.

They walked to an escalator and to a large room. The gentleman stopped just before the door. "On behalf of the airline, we are all terribly sorry for your loss." He paused. "But these folks in here may be able to answer some of your questions." He escorted them into the room. There were people everywhere. Doug noted that some were probably parents, couples, kids, and grandparents. He noted clergy representing many denominations, both standing by and talking to grieving families.

Abbey took one look and stopped in her tracks. Doug waited for her to collect herself and they continued. The gentleman walked them over to a table and waved to one of the ministers.

Doug looked around and saw people crying, wandering, fussing, and some just sitting, staring sadly at nothing.

He waited for the minister to arrive. "Before you begin," Doug said, "I have already talked to my pastor and I don't think there is anything you can say that hasn't already been said." He paused a moment, then said, "I want to talk to someone from the airline!"

The minister quietly agreed. "My brother in Christ, in these times of need, I truly understand and wish that I could help. But right now, I know that your pain is so deeply rooted that there is nothing or no human being that could console your soul. Please." He reached out with some literature. "Please, when you get the time, try and read this." He waited for Doug to accept it, then turned to the next family.

Doug and Abbey waited in the room for a few hours. Doug walked around and looked at all the families that were sharing the same pain as he was. A few minutes later, he returned to Abbey.

"We've waited long enough, let's go home."

CHAPTER 5

"I want to know what happened," Abbey said. "Someone has to come out here and say something."

A few moments later, man from the airline entered and called for attention. "I am the spokesman for the airline. This is really a horrific moment for everyone here. We sympathize and offer our deepest condolences to all the victims and families. There are no words to express our pain and grief. It is saddening. It is simply too much to bear. From what we know at this point, the aircraft lost the number two engine while climbing in altitude. Shortly after the engine failed, the aircraft lost all power and burst into flames right before impact. It landed in a field adjacent to the runway. We still don't know the number of victims on the ground, if any. The debris was scattered over the road and field." He took a breath. "We have yet to differentiate the passengers from any others. All questions will be answered as soon as we have enough information." His eyes scanned the room.

A voice in the background yelled, "Were there any survivors?" Others echoed the question.

"My brother was on that flight."

"Is my mother dead?"

"Can you offer us any hope?"

The representative shook his head. "I'm so sorry. That is all I've been told." He walked out and closed the door behind him.

A woman standing close to Abbey said quietly, "We have been here for the last five hours and that is all that this airline has to say?"

"There has to be someone who knows more about what happened," answered Abbey.

Doug sat patiently for another hour, then stood up and looked to Abbey. "We have been here for too long. Let's go home."

CHAPTER 6

Doug

The house was dark and silent when Doug walked in behind Abbey. The television was off and the deafening sound of Julia playing her music was absent.

I sure wish I could run and tell Julia to turn her music down.

Needing some noise in the too-silent house, Abbey turned the television on and sat on the couch. The news was still covering the airplane crash.

Two men were discussing what happened. They showed illustrations of the path the flight had taken and where it began to descend.

The scene switched to the camera at the scene, which showed the still-smoking wreckage.

The anchormen begin to read the bulletin. "The NTSB located the black box from Flight 1015. And are talking to the airport's air control tower to try and find out more information. Further detail will be forthcoming. We have cameramen at the scene but are only allowed to film certain areas."

Doug brought Abbey a hot cup of tea and sat next to her.

CHAPTER 6

The anchormen continued reporting. "There are graphic pictures of the crash site, some, out of respect for the dead and their families, we cannot show over the air. Here is one witness account of what he saw. Here's Chad Banks, at the scene."

"Chad Banks here at one site of debris. This witness tells his story." He pointed the microphone at an average-looking man. "I just returned home. There was no one left in the church. I suddenly heard something fall on our roof. Something big. I raced out and saw people, even children, running around. And then I heard a loud explosion and a huge smoke cloud. The whole place was covered in black smoke. Then there was another explosion. Everybody, well they were all screaming. I believe I heard about five explosions all totalled."

Chad moved the mic back to himself. The camera zoomed in on his face. "I have another witness who was closer." The camera widened to show a woman in an old house dress standing beside the reporter. "Tell me, what did you see, ma'am?"

She looked at Chad, then began speaking. "The plane touched this tree here." She pointed to a tree behind them. It was missing the top limbs. "And then it went into that there neighborhood. Then came a noise. It sounded like the end of the world, I tell you. *Boom!* I watched the sky for five minutes, not knowing what to do. I wanted to call somebody, but I didn't know who to call. The roof of this here house was also scraped off by the plane." She pointed to a house. The camera panned over to display a house with damage to the roof. "The shock was just too much. Before I could think, I heard two blasts from the plane. Like *ka-pow, ka-pow*. Ya know?"

Doug stood up and walked toward the TV.

"What are you doing? Abbey asked.

"I don't want to hear or see anymore. I am about to change the channel."

He turned the knob and Channel 3 was also televising the accident. He tried turning to another channel, but all channels were reporting the same thing. "Huh. I thought this only happens in political races and things like that," Doug said as he returned to Channel 2. "I don't know if I want to see any more pictures of the wreck."

"I'm sure they will not be showing any victims," Abbey said.

"Well, even so, I don't want to see any pictures. I'm going to the bedroom."

A few minutes later, Abbey walked into the bedroom. Tears were flowing again.

"How are you doing?" Doug asked.

Abbey sat on the end of the bed and grabbed the towel Doug held. He'd been ready to jump in the shower.

"I should have listened to you," Abbey said as she held her face in the towel and sobbed into it.

"What happened?"

"They showed pictures of the crash site, and I saw Chris' helmet. They *showed* the helmet."

Doug went still for a few moments, then he spread out on the bed and invited Abbey to join him. "We need some rest. We've been through a lot today."

CHAPTER 7

Doug

The next day, Doug woke to an empty bed. Abbey had gotten up early. He found her on the couch in the living room, just staring out the window.

"You know... today is the... worst day of my life," she said. Her words came out haltingly and quiet. "I tried to go to sleep last night but I couldn't. The only thing I could think of was my babies, and the last conversations we had before they boarded that airplane. Oh, how I wish I could have that last two hours back." She paused for a few moments, apparently gathering her emotional strength. "I walked into Julia's room this morning and sat on her bed. Her scent there was overwhelming. I grabbed her pillow and lay on her bed." Her voice broke. "Wh-why did this have to happen?"

Doug stood and listened but made no suggestions. He just wanted Abbey to be comfortable talking about the kids. He was shelving his emotions to be strong for her.

"I remember you handing Chris his helmet before he walked away... I can still see his smile as he walked proudly with his sister. He was growing up to be such a wonderful kid. I couldn't make myself enter his room. I tried... but I just couldn't do it." She held out a hand to Doug. "It's just too soon to be able to accept such a terrible thing could happen to my babies."

Doug walked over and sat down next to her.

"Last night, I couldn't think straight, all kinds of things were going through my head. I had thoughts, remembering my last conversation with Julia." Abbey turned to face Doug. "She came to our room and apologized for not wanting to fly alone. And last night, I blamed myself for the whole thing. Doug, I saw it in her eyes. She really didn't want to go. But I kept telling her she'd have fun." Abbey gasped for air at the memory. The guilt. "The pain of our last conversation kept playing in my head and I... I just couldn't get rid of it."

Abbey stood up and walked away.

Doug walked back and started the shower. He looked at the bed and remembered the spot where Chris had jumped and laughed. Slowly, he walked back into the living room. Abbey was in the kitchen on the phone, probably talking to Beth. She whispered her words.

He moved closer to make sure that she was not crying and, if she was, he'd console her.

"I couldn't sleep last night," Abbey said. "And I think Doug feels that it was his fault."

But Doug didn't hear her say *he "feels" like it was his fault*; he only heard *Doug* and *fault*.

He crept closer to the door to hear the rest of the conversation.

As Abbey began to conclude her phone call, Doug walked back to the bedroom, very upset.

He closed the door and took a shower, *his fault. His fault* repeated over and over in his head.

CHAPTER 7

When he walked out of the shower and finished drying himself off, he went into the living room looking for Abbey, but he saw her through the window. She had gone outside and was in the front yard. She returned with roses in her hands. The neighbors had left flowers, candles, cards, and roses in the front yard to show their condolences.

With tears in her eyes, she presented the roses to Doug. "The neighbors held a wake in our front yard, there's cards and flowers."

Doug acknowledged the roses but didn't say a word. He walked away and into the kitchen.

Thinking nothing about it, Abbey found a vase and put the roses on the mantel, next to Julia's and Chris' pictures.

Doug returned empty-handed and looked at Abbey. She was staring at the pictures and roses.

"That was a nice gesture," she said, turning around to Doug. "I wonder when they did that."

"Maybe they brought them after we came into the house from the hotel."

"No, nothing was there when we left last night to go to the airport, and it wasn't there when we returned. I was up all night, and I didn't hear them outside."

Doug walked up to the mantel, touched the roses, and walked away as Abbey stared after him.

"I feel so helpless. I know Doug is hurting as much as I am. I'll just let him have some time to himself." Abbey whispered the words.

Doug turned and walked out of the room and returned with his hat and coat. "I'm going for a ride; I need to be alone for a while." He walked to the door.

Abbey yelled, "That's not fair!"

Doug stopped at the door and hesitated without turning around.

WHOSE FAULT?

Abbey spoke angrily. "You are supposed to be here for me and me for you."

"Fair? What part of this is fair?" Doug opened the door and slammed it behind him.

A few hours later, the doorknob turned, and Doug walked into the house. Abbey was sitting on the couch waiting for him. She sat silently until he entered the living room.

"Our children died yesterday in an airplane crash and today... this is the way you handle it. Being alone?" Her voice revealed the rage inside. "There is so much stuff we have to talk about."

"Stuff to talk about? Like what?" Doug asked.

"Like funeral arrangements, memorials, and who's going to do the eulogy," Abbey said.

Doug huffed. "Well, those things are just going to have to wait until I am physically... emotionally ready," Doug said and headed to their bedroom.

"What do you mean until you are *physically ready*? These things can't wait for you to get yourself together."

Doug went to the bedroom and shut the door.

A few minutes later, Abbey walked in. "What is the matter? With all that is going on, I don't have enough strength to be going through anything else."

Doug sighed and stood up. He slowly walked toward Abbey.

Putting his hands on her shoulders, he explained. "I went and talked to Pastor Andrews. There was something that I had to talk to him about."

Abbey looked at him and shook her head. "I can't believe you went without me. If it was about the kids, then I should have been there with you. Don't exclude me from talks like that. I may need some spiritual guidance myself."

"This was personal. I just needed to get some clarification about... how to proceed. With all that is going on, I can't have

CHAPTER 7

thoughts and words supersede what is important. What is important is preserving my kids' memories."

"What are you talking about?" Abbey burst out, screaming at him.

Doug kept his voice low. "I'm talking about our kids, Abbey." Doug raised his voice. "I'm *talking* about our kids.".

"I know that," Abbey said, staring into Doug's face. "Don't you think it's hurting me just as much as it is hurting you? We should be trying to get through this together instead of apart."

Doug sat back down on the bed and thought for a while.

"If we were going to be dealing with this together, then who were you talking to on the phone earlier?"

Abbey paused for a minute. "My sister Beth. She called, concerned about our wellbeing. She was asking about the kids and wanted to know if we needed for her to come out."

"Is that all you all talked about?"

"What are you getting at? What do you mean?"

"I was at the door and heard you talking on the phone. I just wanted to ask you a question. And I heard you tell your sister that it was *my fault they died*."

"What? When did I say that?"

"Come on, Abbey, I heard you, I was listening."

"No," she said. "You were eavesdropping and overheard wrong."

"Whatever you want to call it, I still heard you say that this was my fault. Why didn't you just tell me how you felt? Hell, if I thought that any of this was any of our faults, I would have said so long ago. I don't have to hold my words in this house."

"But you did confide in someone else." Abbey pointed her finger at him. "I have been trying to get you to talk to me ever since we left the airport and you have been avoiding me."

"That is not true. I have just been supporting you and keeping my thoughts to myself." Doug responded.

WHOSE FAULT?

"Well, still, if you thought more to tell her about what is going on instead of me, then maybe you should have her come here!" Doug shouted. "I am *dealing* with this the best way I can and all you are doing is making it worse."

"Maybe you think that this is my fault," Abbey said.

Doug sat silently, staring at the television. Abbey walked over to Doug and stood there looking down on him.

"Is that what this is all about? Is that what you really went and talked to the pastor about?"

Doug never looked up.

"Damn!" Abbey stalked into the kitchen.

She started talking loudly to herself and then started throwing dishes against the kitchen walls.

Doug ran into the kitchen. "What the hell is wrong with you?" He grabbed her arm, loaded with a plate ready to throw.

Abbey stopped and stared at him. "What's wrong? *What's wrong?* My children are dead! That's what is wrong with me. And all you can do is blame me for the whole thing. Okay, so it was me who wanted to spend time with my husband. *It was me* who wanted to have the kids go to my sister's and spend a few days. It all on me." She pulled at her hair out of frustration. "Me, me, me. *I caused this.* All of it."

Doug just stood there, listening. Waiting for her to get it out.

"So, you agree… this is my fault, right? I'm the one that bought the tickets. Kissed the kids goodbye and just left the airport all by myself. You had absolutely nothing to do with this at all, right?"

"Well, I tried to stop it. I wanted them to stay home. You kept making me feel guilty about not spending time with you," Doug said.

Abbey screamed, "You are the one that came into this house and said you needed time away from that job and for me to get the tickets! This is just as much your fault as it is mine, except

CHAPTER 7

you don't want to take responsibility for your part. I guess it's easier for you to accept the outcome if you can just exempt yourself from your part in this."

"Alright!" Doug shouted. "That's enough! I wanted to go with the kids, but you couldn't get the days off, probably never even tried. You just wanted time away from the kids. Well, now you have all the time you want!" Doug shouted and stormed out of the kitchen.

Abbey sat in the kitchen for a while and then walked out to the family room and into the bedroom without looking at Doug.

She slammed the door and turned off the light.

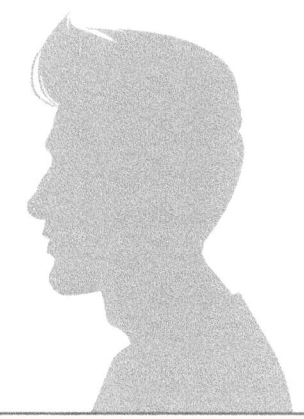 

CHAPTER 8

Doug

The next day, Doug woke up on the couch. He'd tried to get into the bedroom, but the door was locked. He called to Abbey, but she didn't answer.

"I need to get in there to take a shower," he said a little louder, but still no answer. He grabbed the knob again and shook it. "Are you in there?" he asked again, a bit louder.

Still no answer.

Worried, he started knocking on the door aggressively. "Open the door!" But still nothing happened.

He walked around the house to make sure that she was not anywhere else then returned to the door. He grabbed and put all his weight on the door and pushed the door. The door swung open, and Doug walked in quickly.

Abbey was lying still under the covers.

"Abbey!" Doug yelled. He walked closer to the bed.

She moved a leg.

"Abbey!" Doug yelled again.

She blinked and looked up at Doug.

CHAPTER 8

"Are you alright?" he asked.

She rubbed her eyes and stretched. "Yes, I'm fine, physically. I took some relaxers to make myself go to sleep. I haven't really slept since the accident."

Abbey sat up on her side of the bed, facing away from Doug. "So now what?" she asked.

"What do you mean?"

"Last night, you accused me of telling Beth that all of this was your fault. So, I'm asking you… what now?"

"I don't know what now," Doug answered. "I know what I heard, but if you don't feel like you and I can have an honest conversation, then, well, what is the use of continuing the conversation?"

Abbey turned, facing him. "Doug, honestly, why would I have said something like that?"

"Maybe because that is the way you feel," Doug said as he sat on the opposite side of the bed, facing away from Abbey.

"I don't know whose fault this is," Abbey insisted.

"Why does this even have to be anyone's fault?" Doug said, his voice rising. "Just the thought of you thinking that way makes me more assured that you said that to your sister."

Abbey stood up and grabbed the telephone. "We can call her right now. I'll dial the number and you can ask the question."

"Now why would your sister tell me anything that you two talked about? That makes no sense."

Abbey sat back down on the bed, facing away from Doug, and mumbled.

"You can say it out loud," Doug said. "There is nothing that hasn't already been said." He waited a moment. "But I do believe that you are the one that suggested we send the kids to your sister, and you are the one that decided that you wanted them to fly. And I honestly think that you didn't try hard enough to get the days off so that we could have flown with them."

"Finish, Doug!" Abbey yelled. "Go on and get it out."

Doug hesitated.

Abbey began to yell again. "You are the one who came home from work talking about how tired you were and that you needed time away from that job and insisted that I go and buy the tickets. And since we are being brutally honest, you had a chance to cancel all this when Julia came into the room and talked to you. You could have told her that since she was uncomfortable that we decided to cancel the trip. But no, you started thinking about ways to have fun. You started planning stuff. The French Quarter and dinner, a hotel stay for the weekend. Yeah, blame me, Doug. You go right ahead and blame me for what has happened." She sat down violently on the bed, then stood back up and ripped the blinds open. "I'll be damned if I'm going to take all the blame for the death of our children." She stared out the window for a few minutes then quickly walked out the room.

She turned around and returned and stood in the doorway. "Are you sure that's all you did was go and talk to the pastor? Or did you go and tell him that you thought it was my fault they died? There had to have been a reason that you didn't want me there."

Abbey stared angrily at him. She waited for him to say something, then shook her head and walked away.

Several minutes later, Doug walked into the living room. Abbey was standing in the open doorway, looking out into the front yard.

"You know it's funny. I look out to the yard and there are a bunch of flowers that are there in remembrance of our kids. It's nice and quiet out there, peaceful and beautiful. When I turn

CHAPTER 8

around, all I see is a man accusing me of murdering my own children."

Doug stopped in the middle of the room. "You said that, not me."

"Then what are all the accusations about?" Abbey asked.

Doug walked back and sat down, "Look at us. We are at each other's throats and we haven't even laid our kids down to rest. We haven't made any funeral arrangements."

"I tried to talk to you about that yesterday, but you didn't want to hear it," Abbey said.

She slowly closed the door on the outside world. "If for nothing else but Julia and Chris' sake, we could sit down for a few hours and arrange a date and funeral services. Now that we both understand how each other feels about the accident, we should stop fighting and act like adults and give our children a decent burial."

"I'll call the mortuary," Doug said as he stood up. "There is no need for caskets since we don't even have their bodies to bury." Doug stopped for a while and sat back down. "I never in my life thought that I would be making these arrangements. They are supposed to be making these for me."

Abbey walked over to Doug. "I'm sorry for the last few hours." She handed Doug some tissue. "It's just so... hard."

"Maybe we should invite Pastor Andrews over or go to the church and have him give us some spiritual guidance. Counselling. *Whatever.*"

Abbey nodded. "Instead of beating each other down and pointing fingers, we need to be thinking of our babies."

"That's a positive thought." Doug agreed. "And I'm sure he doesn't mind us having their services at the church. I'll call him after I call the mortuary and get everything started."

CHAPTER 9

Abbey and Doug

Abbey and Doug walked into the pastor's chambers and sat down. The pastor was silently reading a scripture. He finished and silently put his Bible on the desk. "Well, Deacon Campbell and Mrs. Campbell, I'm glad that you two could make it here. I am sure you have a lot of questions, so let's get started. First of all, I would like to begin by reading a passage from the good book." He turned to a select page and began reading. "Matthew 19:14. 'But Jesus said, "Let the little children come to me and do not hinder them, for to such belongs the kingdom of heaven."'"

Pastor Andrews stood up and walked behind their chairs. "Deacon Campbell, you said something very interesting while I was visiting you the day of the accident. You said, 'I hope this is not a test of my faith.' I surely empathized with the way you were feeling and would have probably felt the same. The loss of or the death of children is to an adult, backwards, *per se*. I mean it is supposed to be the other way around. So, to say that your faith was being tested is not the way God intended for this to be. Our

CHAPTER 9

God may be a jealous God, but He is surely not a callous God. Of course, He wants us to obey Him and only Him." Pastor Andrews sat back down and turned a few pages. "Here is another verse we can draw strength from. Deuteronomy 6:4-9 tells us, 'Hear, O Israel: The LORD our God, the LORD is one. You shall love the LORD your God with all your heart and with all your soul and with all your might. And these words that I command you today shall be on your heart. You shall teach them diligently to your children and shall talk of them when you sit in your house, and when you walk by the way, and when you lie down, and when you rise. You shall bind them as a sign on your hand, and they shall be as frontlets between your eyes. You shall write them on the doorposts of your house and on your gates.'"

He looked up to them. "No one can feel the pain in your hearts right now, except God. I don't have the words to express what's going on in your hearts, but from a mere glance, I can see the pain on both of your faces. But you had two *wonderful* God-fearing children. They were at Sunday school every Sunday. They believed in our Lord and Father. There is no human soul on this earth that can come up with a reason why Julia and Chris were taken away from you. That was God's choice. He called them home *to be with Him*."

Abbey lowered her head, staring at the floor.

"Is there something that you want to say, Abbey?" Pastor Andrews asked.

Abbey paused and then looked at Doug. "I am sure that you don't have the answer to my question, but I will ask it anyway. Why *my children*, what did they or I do that would make God call them home? They were babies. *Our babies.*"

"That's a very good question indeed, Abbey, but one that has been asked over a million times and has the same answer today. And that is there is no answer to that question. As humans or in the biblical sense, we don't have the power, if I can use that word, to question God. All we can do is pray for the answers. Pray for His mercy, His guidance, His grace."

"I have prayed, cried, gotten angry, frustrated and even felt like taking my own life," Abbey said. "I feel so empty without my children. They were the essence of my life." She grabbed some tissues from her purse and started wiping at the tears falling off her cheeks.

Silence weighed heavy in the room as Doug attended to Abbey.

"So, Doug, what about you? Is there something you would like to ask?"

"I have pretty much felt the same way as my wife. I have been reading the Bible to try to make some kind of sense of this. But my concentration is always disturbed by wanting my kids with me again. I can't concentrate without talking to my kids or wanting them to just appear. Like it was all a bad dream." He shook his head. "When I said to you that I hope that this is not a test of my faith, I was emotionally out of my mind. I don't even remember driving home. I don't remember stopping at any red lights, I don't even remember getting on or off the freeway. Everything since I read and saw the words on that television in the French Quarter, everything is a blur. I can't concentrate or go to work right now. I am an angry man."

"That's normal. You should feel angry, but less upset as a Christian. You know that your children are with our God, right now. As a man of the cloth, as you are, you should understand the meaning of what has taken place." Pastor Andrews said, trying to convince them both to use their understanding. And rely on and trust their faith.

Doug stood up and paced the floor, looking for words to express his feelings. He stopped behind Abbey and put his hands on her shoulders. "But Pastor, I am also a husband and

CHAPTER 9

father, and fathers hurt like mothers. Because I am a deacon doesn't take any of the pain or the burdens away. I am a man with a family and that only comes second to what I do here at church. I have my Bible at home stuck on the verse that I have tried to live my life by."

"And what is that verse?" Pastor Andrews asked.

Doug walked around and held on to the pastor's Bible. He turned a few pages, knowing exactly where the scripture was.

"Here." He handed the Bible back to Pastor Andrews.

"No, Deacon, you go on ahead and read it for us."

Deacon Campbell reached for the Bible and cleared his throat. "Ephesians 5:22, 28-31. 'Wives submit yourselves unto your own husbands, as unto the Lord. For the husband is head of the wife and children, even as Christ is head of the church; and he is the savior of the body. Therefore, as the church is subject to Christ, so let wives be to their own husbands in everything. Husbands love your wife and children as Christ also loved the church and gave himself for it . . . So, ought men to love their wives and children as their own bodies. He that loveth his wife and children loveth himself. For no man ever yet hated his own flesh but nourisheth and cherisheth it, even as the Lord the church . . . For this cause shall a man leave his father and mother and shall be joined unto his wife, and they two shall be one flesh.'"

"Oh yes, that is a great scripture," Pastor Andrews said. "I see you even added a few words to make it fit your situation. Remember this scripture as you leave and go home." He turned and walked around to stand next to the both of them. "1 Corinthians 10:13, 'There hath no temptation taken you, but such as is common to man: but God is faithful, who will not suffer you to be tempted above that ye are able; but will with the temptation also make a way to escape, that ye may be able to bear it.'

It's more often said like this, *God would never put more on you than you can't handle.*'" He paused a moment. "So, when is the funeral?" Pastor Andrews asked.

"We were thinking about this Sunday and were going to ask if we could have it here at the church."

"Of course, you should have it here. This was their church home, they were members of this church, and they were also baptized here."

Abbey stood up and offered her hand to Doug. "We would also ask that you do the eulogy."

"Absolutely, it would be a privilege. I would take it as an honor to send those children's souls to God." Pastor Andrews waited in silence to see if there were any more requests. After a brief silence, he spoke. "I guess this is the conclusion of this counseling session." He offered up a short prayer. "He healeth the broken in heart, and bindeth up their wounds, Psalms 147:3."

"I will be looking forward to seeing you two on Wednesday."

Pastor Andrew walked them to the car and waited for them to drive away, then returned to the church.

CHAPTER 10

Abbey

The rays from the sun penetrated through the curtains, prematurely awakening Abbey from her sleep. She looked and noticed that Doug had already left the bedroom. She walked slowly out of the room, putting her gown on. Doug was at the dining table. "Good morning," she said.

"Today is Sunday," Doug said, "and right now I don't know what kind of day it is going to be. I do know that it is going to be the hardest day of my life."

Abbey sat down across from him.

Doug continued. "Today, I get to bury my children. That is the kind of day I am going to have. If any little girl or boy deserved to finish living out their dreams, it had to be those two. They were the perfect children, never gave us any real problems past the normal growing up process." He held the obituary up and let it drop, gently hitting the table. "But they are gone just the same, right now, I don't even like going outdoors because I find myself wishing that someone else's kids were dead and mine were still alive. And I know it is wrong to feel that way, but that is the way I feel."

Abbey sat in the chair and let Doug finish his thoughts.

"I don't even get to see them again… just empty coffins and memories are all I have left."

"But you do have memories," Abbey said. "You have very fond memories of them growing up. For seventeen years, I watched as you stood over Julia with your chest puffed out. You are a proud father." She took his hand. "And with the hard pregnancy that I had with her, I knew that you wanted another child. So, God gave us Chris. When you found out that your child was going to be a boy, my, how your smile made me know that we had done the right thing."

Doug grabbed the obituary again and began rubbing the pictures. "If only I could tell them one more time how much I love them. If only I could have been there with them to at least try to guard them or comfort them. Then, they wouldn't have died alone. I have dreams of what they were going through during their last minutes and it is horrifying. Every time I close my eyes… I see Chris coming back… for his helmet." Doug broke down into a deep cry.

"Go on and get this off your chest," Abbey said. "Get it all out. Just cry." Abbey walked over to him and began caressing his shoulders. "It's going to be alright. They are in a place where they can't be harmed ever again."

"And I have to believe that, too," Abbey said. She continued caressing his shoulders.

The doorbell rang, Doug walked into the family room. Abbey walked to the door and was surprised when Beth walked in, followed by her husband.

"Where is Doug?" Beth asked.

"He is sitting over there, in the other room."

CHAPTER 10

"How are you holding up? I know I should have gotten here a few days ago but my job just would not allow me to leave."

"I understand," Abbey said.

"So what time are the services? I know we were cutting it real close."

"You are here just in time to wait for me and Doug to go and get dressed." Abbey waited for Doug to come in, then walked with him back to their bedroom.

They both got dressed silently, thinking of the arguments they had a few days ago and Beth being just the person that could eventually clear everything up. Abbey finished first and walked towards the door. She looked back to see if Doug was finishing up.

Doug looked at her and she knew what he was thinking. But neither said a word.

Doug stood up and began picking at his pants to get the lint off. Finally, he broke the silence. "At least you now have someone to lean on when it gets tough in there."

"Well," Abbey said, "Nathan is there, too."

"Yes, he is, but we are not as close as you and your sister, and besides, the only time we really say anything to each other is when we are talking about the both of you."

Abbey, sensing where this was going, grabbed the doorknob and opened the door. "We are going to be late if we don't leave now."

Nathan was at the door. "Is there going to be a limousine here to pick you two up?"

"No, we decided to drive to the church ourselves and to the gravesite."

They all walked out of the house together. "Here," Nathan said, "I will drive." Doug hesitated then handed the keys to him and walked around to the passenger side of the car.

They arrived at the church and Pastor Andrews was standing at the door welcoming each and every person to the service. He saw them approaching and yelled to one of his Deacons. "Deacon Campbell's car should be parked right in front of the church, next to the two hearses."

As soon as Abbey saw the hearses, she gasped and immediately turned to Beth.

Pastor Andrews walked around opened the door and reached for her hand. "It's all in God's hands now."

Beth got out of the car on the opposite side and quickly walked around to Abbey and caught hold of her hand. "Let's go and give our babies to God," she whispered. "I know this is very hard, but it is very necessary."

Doug and Nathan walked in behind them and up to the front of the church.

Pastor Andrews began the services by identifying the deceased, and then identifying the parents and loved ones.

When he finished the eulogy, everyone in the church was weeping.

At the gravesite, after the pastor finished the graveside services, he looked at Doug. "I believe you wanted this time."

Doug walked up to the casket and placed the football tickets on Chris' casket and walked away. He held on to Abbey as they began to lower the two caskets into the ground simultaneously.

He grabbed Abbey. "Let's go. I don't want to see this part." Abbey stood still and watched until they were finished. Beth stood next to her until she was ready to leave.

The ride home was somber, no one said a word and the radio was off. The car turned the corner slowly approaching the house. "Stop! I want to walk the rest of the way," Abbey said.

CHAPTER 10

Nathan pulled over and Abbey got out of the car, she stumbled a little getting out and Doug got out and rushed to her side.

"You two go on ahead," Doug said. "We will be there shortly."

Nathan slowly pulled away and, a few minutes later, pulled into the driveway.

Abbey walked slowly with Doug holding her hand. "We have lived in this neighborhood for twenty-one years, and this the first time I have walked this street without at least one of our children with me."

They got closer to the house and neighbors and friends drifted out and walked with them. When they arrived home, they had fifteen to twenty neighbors with them. Abbey hugged everyone and Doug shook hands with all the gentlemen and then they walked into the house.

Beth was in the kitchen cleaning when Abbey walked in. "Oh, you don't have to do that," Abbey said.

Beth looked at Abbey. "You look like you haven't slept in days. Go on and take a nap."

"I feel fine," Abbey demanded. "And I can clean up just fine."

Beth stood firmly to her guns. "I will handle this. Now you go and get some rest. Let me do this small thing for you."

Abbey, not wanting to fuss, just walked away and into the bedroom. Doug was in the room sitting on the bed when she entered.

"Why are you sitting in the dark?" she asked. She walked towards the switch.

"Please don't turn on that light, *please*," he begged.

"Are you okay?" Abbey asked.

"Not really." Doug sat still.

Abbey walked over to him and noticed that Doug had something in his hand. "What do you have in your hand?" Abbey asked, concerned.

WHOSE FAULT?

"It's not what you think." He paused. "I have these." He raised his hand, which held two pictures. One of Julia and one of Chris. "I don't know how to continue. I have tried to pray for the answers, but I am not getting any answers. Feels like I am losing my mind. I have lost my kids, argued with my wife... nothing makes sense anymore. I just keep wishing it were all a bad dream."

"What are you talking about Doug? You haven't said much to me... really since our disagreement."

"We've talked," Doug said and turned around. "I have been speaking to you. We went and seen the pastor, remember?"

"Yes, but when we left, I felt like there was something else you wanted to talk to him about while we were there."

"That's not true. I said everything I wanted to say to him."

"Then why are you so quiet? Sitting in the dark all by yourself."

"Just thinking to myself... praying. Asking for strength. Asking for my children back." Doug stood up and walked toward the door, then he glanced back to Abbey. "I'm going for a drive."

Abbey sat watching as he walked out the door. She returned to the kitchen and began drying the dishes as Beth washed them.

"Is there something wrong?" Beth asked. "Other than the obvious, I mean."

Abbey stood silently, continuing to dry the dishes.

Beth stopped and dried her hands. "Look, you have been through the most devastating time a woman can ever go through."

Abbey walked away and sat down. "I don't know what to do."

"What do you mean?" Beth asked.

"I've lost my kids and now I think I am losing my husband. I think he blames me for them being on that airplane. He says he heard you and me talking... says we blame him for them being there."

"What!" Beth shrieked.

CHAPTER 10

"Yes, when we were talking on the phone, he overheard me say *blame*, but he never heard the whole conversation."

"Well, I will talk to him when he returns," Beth said fiercely.

Abbey looked at her. "With that attitude, he will only think we are trying to hide something. He knows you'd be loyal to me."

"Well, he needs to know that we were not saying that, and I mean to tell him just that."

"I don't want him thinking that about me, especially not about this."

"We have had a very good relationship up to now, even though I didn't like him when you two first met."

The front door opened and closed.

"Okay, there he is. Do you mind if I go and have a talk with him?" Beth asked.

"I don't know if that is the right thing to do just now," Abbey said.

"Well, big sister, someone needs to go and say something to him. Well, maybe I can talk to Nathan and see if he could talk to him."

"That might help, but tell him not to pry too hard. I don't want to start another argument like—" Abbey caught herself.

"Start an argument like what?" Beth asked. "Have you two been arguing?"

"We've had one heated conversation about what he *thought* he heard me say over the phone."

"Did you two get physical?"

"No, we never let anything physical happen. After all, he is my husband, and I am his wife."

"Whatever that means." Beth waved a hand and left the room to find Nathan. She walked right past Doug and never said a word. "Hey baby, can I talk to you?" She looked around to make sure there was no one around. "I need you to try and talk to Doug."

"Sure. Talk to him about what?" Nathan asked curiously.

"I need you to talk to him just to see if he would talk about what happened here."

"Wait a minute," Nathan said. He walked closer to Beth. "I don't want to pry into their business, I came here to support them not get involved in their affairs. And I have no idea what happened. I probably don't want to know."

"I understand that because I don't want to get involved either, but they do not agree about what happened."

"And that really has nothing to do with us Beth," Nathan said.

"I just want him to talk," Beth said. "Go in there and try and talk about anything, see if he wants to talk. Act normal."

Nathan snorted. "Alright, I'll try to *act normal.*" He used air quotes. "But if he isn't wanting to talk, I'm not going to force anything."

Nathan walked around to find Doug, who had gone to the bedroom.

He went back to Beth. "I'm going to wait till he comes out of his room, I'm not going in there and invade his personal space. That's just not *normal.*" Again, the air quotes popped up.

Beth grinned and punched him in the arm. "Okay, smarty-pants, I'll go back and check on Abbey."

Nathan walked back into the living room and sat down to read a magazine. A few minutes later, Doug walked in.

Nathan stood up. "Are you okay, man?"

Doug stopped and looked around the room, then made eye contact. "Yeah, I think I'm okay, just a little thirsty."

"Well, how about we go and grab a beer?"

Doug hesitated and shook his head. "No, I think I will just have some water."

"Well, what if I go on down and grab a six-pack and bring it back? We can sit in the backyard and watch the sky."

CHAPTER 10

"That sounds a little better," Doug said and began reaching into his pocket.

"I've got this," Nathan said and walked out the door.

As soon as the door shut, Abbey and Beth quickly walked into the living room.

They noticed Doug and no Nathan... Abbey looked at Beth, concerned.

"Where is Nathan?" Beth asked, walking to look out the window.

"He went on down to the store, and he'll be back."

Beth grabbed a fist full of curtain and peeked out.

"He *went* to the *store*," Doug repeated, enunciating his words carefully.

Beth glanced at Doug.

"Is there something wrong? You're acting a bit... *squirrely*," Doug said smartly.

"Oh?" Beth asked. "More than usual?"

Abbey walked over behind Doug and cut her eyes to Beth. She jerked her head, silently telling Beth to go back to the kitchen.

She put her arms around Doug's shoulders. "I'm worried about you."

Doug waited a heartbeat and then stood to return to the bedroom. He stopped. "I am angry right now. I'm doing my best, but I really don't want to talk to anyone."

"You are angry about what?" Abbey begged.

"Have you forgotten already what has transpired around here?" he asked suddenly. "Have you gotten over the kids being gone already? Have you forgotten we buried *our children* today? He screamed, "Well, I haven't! I am angry because they are gone, I am angry because I haven't had the time to mourn the deaths of both my children."

"Who are you mad at?" Abbey yelled back.

Doug stared at her for a while, closed his eyes, and turned toward the bedroom.

Just then, Nathan walked into the house, and looked around, knowing that he had just either missed something or interrupted something.

He glanced over at Abbey. "Did I interrupt something?" He sat the bag down on the table and looked around for Beth.

"She is in the kitchen," Doug said, "and can you tell her to come in here? I need to get this over with. I am holding on to something that needs to be in the open." Doug began pacing the floor waiting for them to return.

"What is this all about?" Abbey asked.

Doug paced silently and didn't answer.

Nathan and Beth walked in. Beth glanced nervously over to Abbey. "Is this about what I think it is about?" she asked.

"What do you think this is about?" Doug asked.

"Well, if it's about me and my sister's conversation over the phone last week, then it went exactly how she said it went. Doug, *nobody* blamed you for this terrible accident."

"So, you two have been talking behind my back, which is very comforting to hear, especially knowing my wife is involved."

"Wait a minute," Abbey said as she stood up. "You just wait a minute. It wasn't just my idea for the kids to be on that damn airplane. It was just as much your choice as it was mine. We both wanted to spend time with each other and now all the damn accusations?"

"I don't deserve this and especially coming from you," Doug said. "I am in just as much pain as you are, except you need to try to take blame or responsibility off yourself. I am not trying to avoid my part. I'm just trying to make sense of God's decision."

Nathan just sat and stared at both of them.

CHAPTER 10

Beth interrupted. "I thought both of you were church-going and God-fearing people." She looked at Doug. "And you are a deacon, for God's sake."

Doug turned to face her quickly. "And what does that have to do with the death of my children? Am I not supposed to hurt because God took my kids? Am I not supposed to mourn the loss of my children?"

He walked away, grabbed the Bible, and then returned back to them. "I have been studying this Bible for most of my life and I have never read a scripture that says I shouldn't hurt or mourn. I have had meetings with our pastor and that isn't helping."

Beth waited for him to finish his rant. "Well, maybe you should allow your wife to help you through this, what about that?" She walked up to him, then turned and faced Abbey. "What happened to for richer and for poorer, in sickness and in health? Huh? What happened to all that? Were those just pretty words? What happened to supporting and cherishing her in prosperity and in trouble?" She looked at each of them. "I am not on either of your sides and I mean it. Yes, you have had a very bad experience. Yes, you have had a terrible loss. No! Your children are not here anymore, but they are only gone in the flesh. What do you think they are thinking right now, watching you two tear each other up? Who are the children now? Remember it's the duty of both of you to find the greatest joy in the company of each other and to remember that in interest and in affection you are to be henceforth one and undivided." She paused for a moment. "So, what happened to all that?" She looked around and waited for a response. "Come on Nathan, let's go on home; I want to catch the first thing smoking back to Chicago."

As soon as the door closed, Abbey walked quickly into the kitchen and Doug made a beeline to the bedroom.

CHAPTER 11

Abbey

The next morning after sleeping on the couch, Abbey walked into the bedroom to take a shower.

Doug was lying in the bed, watching the news on television.

She got just past the bathroom door and turned around. "So, are you satisfied?"

Doug continued watching television without paying any attention to her.

Abbey walked over to the TV and turned it off. "I asked you a question."

"What was the question?" Doug sighed.

Abbey repeated. "I asked if you were you satisfied."

Doug's voice showed his irritation. "Am I satisfied about what?"

Abbey took a few steps toward Doug. "About what was said last night. I told you that I didn't say you were to blame. So, are you satisfied?"

Doug sat up in the bed, all the while looking at her.

"What did you just say?" he asked. "You asked me if I am satisfied?

CHAPTER 11

"Are you kidding me? This is not just about that. It's about so much more than last night."

Doug stood up. "If you want me to say that you were right, then here it is. You were right. Now how does that make you feel? Do you feel better? Is your situation any better now than a few minutes ago?"

Doug continued, "I will admit I was wrong, but not about that. I was wrong because I didn't fight hard enough for my daughter. I didn't listen to her wishes. She told me that she didn't want to go, and I still sent her. I have to live with that reality for the rest of my life. So, you go on and bask in your win. Because honestly, from where I stand, you may have won this little argument, but the biggest prize was lost. I was wrong because my kid asked for my help, and I… didn't give her the time or the attention she was asking for. In my time of grief, I heard something you said, and it could have been because of the pain I was in or that I wanted it to sound like you were blaming me. But now that I look back on it, it was my anguish that was controlling my thoughts and wanted me to want someone to tell me it was my fault."

Abbey stared at Doug. "The pain and misery you are in, I am in also. And I would have never said that about you. You have been such a great father to those children that it would have been such a travesty to have said that about you. I know your pain; I feel it every time I wake up or see something that belongs to one of them. I can't escape the heartache and pain when I play that conversation with Julia again and again in my head. I kick myself each and every time I think of what I was doing instead of *listening*." Abbey lowered her head and walked into the bathroom. That thought, that conversation, replayed in her head over and over again.

Doug turned back around to sit on the bed and then spun around again. "Last night, I came in there to read you this scripture from the Bible." He cleared his throat and began to read. "*Ephesians 4:26, Be angry and do not sin; do not let the sun go down on your anger.* But you had already gone to sleep. I still read the Bible and still believe in its words. Last night I finally got the courage to walk into the kids' rooms. I haven't been in there since the day they left. I couldn't care less about last night and all that was said."

Abbey put her towel down on the bathroom sink and walked out of the bathroom.

"I have wondered what you were thinking about and were you thinking like I was. Silently I was blaming myself for our kids leaving. But it bothered me that we were fighting each other and not really discussing anything of substance, just angry words. All those meetings that we have had with Pastor Andrews were going right out the window because of our anger. But then I think to myself, would any other couple be going through the same things we were going through?"

"Possibly, but people handle things so very differently." Doug stood up and walked over to Abbey. "In hindsight, I don't think you would have said that about me, but I needed a reason to fuss. To show my frustration."

Abbey sat down on the bed. "I felt like just throwing it all away, and I mean everything. And I think if you hadn't fought so hard, I would have given up."

Doug nodded. "Me too. I was reeling and feeling awful about the whole situation."

Abbey stood up and hugged Doug tight. "We have an appointment with the pastor this evening." Doug pulled away slowly. Abbey waited. "Today is our scheduled meeting day. We only have a few appointments left.'

Doug grabbed his jacket and walked out the door alongside her.

CHAPTER 11

Doug walked into the church just behind Abbey.

"Well," Pastor Andrews said. He stepped away from the piano. "I was just finishing up the music for our new hymn. Did you hear the music?"

"Yes," Abbey said, nodding her head. "I did and it sounded so nice."

"Well, now all I have to do is find the right voice to go with the music and lyrics." Pastor Andrews began walking towards the offices. "Would you please join me?"

He closed the door as Doug followed Abbey in and sat down.

"Today I am not going to be sitting down, no, today, I am going to stand up," he said.

Abbey looked at Doug with questioning eyebrows.

"What was that about?" Pastor Andrews asked her.

"Nothing really, just wondering where you are going with this."

"Well, yesterday I had a very interesting visitor come here to the church."

Doug and Abbey looked at each other, wondering who he was referring to.

"Yes, the visitor wanted me to know something about the two of you."

"Who was it? Who came here?" They spoke simultaneously.

Pastor Andrews walked around to his chair and stood just behind it. He stared at them. "You two should be ashamed of yourselves. But here's the problem that I have. On one hand, I really can't feel what you two are probably still feeling. If you have not been there, then you really shouldn't try to understand what the healing process should be."

"What are you talking about?" Doug asked.

WHOSE FAULT?

Pastor Andrews looked at Doug. "You are a deacon at this church and your behavior towards one of our ushers was unacceptable."

Doug thought for a minute and was about to answer when Abbey asked, "My sister was here wasn't she?"

"Yes, she was, Abbey, and she sat here with her husband and practically begged me to go to your house. And for a minute, I was going to do just that. Then I thought that it was a family issue and that I really had no business barging into your home and saying anything. But now that we are here, on a level playing field, so to speak, I can now give you God's words in terms of what you are going through. But before I start, I would like to speak from the heart and not the Bible."

Pastor Andrews walked around and stood behind them. "You two have been married for a long, long time. I should know, I was the person who performed the wedding. I have had deep respect for both of you. That is why I had accepted your invitation to counsel you two on your relationship. You two have been members of this church since I decided to minister here. You even let me baptize your children, so in saying that, I feel like I am a part of your extended family. But that doesn't give me the right to always speak out of turn. But if you don't ever listen to me speak another word, please hear me now. You can survive this, but it is going to take some divine intervention. It's going to take some deep understanding and listening. I know it's hard to comprehend right now but you are going to have to depend on each other to get through this. There's going to be good days and then there are going to be very bad days. But watching the kids grow and knowing you two, I am sure that you have some very fond and precious memories of them.

Pastor Andrews paused, looking like he wanted clarity of his words. "My definition of memory is this. The ability of the brain

CHAPTER 11

to retain and to use the knowledge gained from past experiences. Now, I am sure you have some very treasured memories of those kids," Pastor Andrews repeated again. He touched them both on the shoulders. "They were your joy, now just remember where they are at this moment." He smiled. "That's right. They are in the arms of Jesus, our Lord." He took a moment to let that sink in. "Now, here is what the Bible says about what you are going through." Pastor Andrews walked around the desk and finally sat down. He began thumbing through the pages. He looked over his eyeglasses and smiled. "Aaahh, here is what I've been searching for." He read aloud. *"Matthew 5:14. Blessed are those who mourn, for they will be comforted."*

He straightened himself up in the chair and looked at both of them. "In this scripture, I believe that God is looking down on you and He sees your pain. He may not like the way you two are handling your situation, I mean, *blaming each other?*" He clucked his tongue. "Tsk-tsk." He continued. "But still, your sorrows will be comforted. The fact that the kids are with Him speaks volumes. And the truth to the matter is that it really doesn't matter what the kids were doing at that time… it was their time to depart this life, so if you two are questioning each other about whose fault it is that your kids are gone, then you must first consult the Bible and know that God absolutely, one hundred percent, doesn't make mistakes."

He looked at Abbey. "So, what made you think it was Doug's fault?"

Abbey turned and looked at Doug. "I have never said that it was your fault, I believe it was insinuated that I said that. And before I could explain what was really said, you had already started your tantrum. I thought you were disrespectful and trying to make me upset. I also believe that if Beth had not said what she said in our living room, we would not be here at this time. She collected all of our skeletons and brought them to life. As my husband and me being your wife, I think we should have handled this differently. I still love you so much and this has made me realize how much I do love you. Some couples would argue to the point of saying things they can't take back. I know it was pain that was the reason we were acting this way and I wholeheartedly forgive you for your part in this." She looked over at Doug, who had tears falling from his face. She reached for him for a hug.

Pastor Andrews turned to Doug. "And Deacon Campbell, what made you think this was Abbey's fault?"

Doug collected himself, turned to Abbey, and spoke. "First of all, I don't recollect ever saying this was your fault. I did, however, come very close, but the words of *fault* were never spoken. I felt slighted when I overheard your conversation and really thought you had said it was my fault and, like I have said before, maybe I was misguided by my anger." Doug hesitated, shrugged his shoulders, and then continued. "God, how I loved those children and maybe you needed them far more than we did. But you have taken two true angels. Sometimes we don't understand Your wisdom… but now is not the time to question but a time to mourn. I hope that my wife can forgive my behavior over the last few days and truly understand that the loss of my children was the reason for that. I want to take this time to send out a prayer for Beth, she opened our closed eyes. She made Abbey and me realize that through all this, we still have each other and should lean on each other's strengths instead of arguing over something we can't change. I have vowed to love my wife no matter what and that is what I intend to do. We have so much to be thankful for, we have memories of our kids and that is something that no one can ever take away from us. The healing process will

CHAPTER 11

continue when we leave this church, but now, we can begin to mourn correctly instead of fighting each other."

Pastor Andrews grabbed his Bible. "Wonderful. Here is one last scripture that I want you both to leave with. *Revelations 21:4. 'He will wipe away every tear from their eyes, and death shall be no more, neither shall there be mourning, nor crying, nor pain anymore, for the former things have passed away.'"*

Pastor Andrews walked to the door and waited for the both of them to exit. "I hope today's session has brought the both of you a deeper understanding and given you some closure."

He waited for them to reach their car. "Go on home and apply today's lesson to your everyday lives. Life is so precious, and we should cherish our time here for no one knows of the hour to be your last."

CHAPTER 12

Abbey and Doug

Abbey and Doug walked into the house after the meeting with Pastor Andrews; Abbey waited for Doug and then closed the door. No one said a word. Doug walked into the kitchen and Abbey into the bedroom. She began making the bed, picked up a corner of the mattress to tuck the sheet and felt a piece of paper. She grabbed the paper, which was actually an envelope, opened it and grabbed the contents. Her knees buckled and she practically fell onto the bed.

Doug walked in just as she sat down. "What is it?"

She began to slide the papers out of the envelope. It was Julia's eleventh-grade pictures.

Doug slowly took the pictures and sat down next to her.

"These are the pictures she said she didn't like and wanted to take them over, but we never received the makeover date and she decided to hide them so that I wouldn't send them to friends and family. She put them in the one place that she thought I wouldn't look," Abbey explained. "She absolutely hated these pictures," Abbey said, smiling. "And I never said anything about

CHAPTER 12

them to her. She was so adamant about taking more pictures that when we figured that there would be no more pictures taken at school, she wanted to take some at the mall studio. She was so particular about the way she presented herself to the public and especially at school."

Doug handed the pictures back to Abbey. "She was such a beautiful young lady. Ever since I was a young man, I have always wanted a set of bookends. I finally got them and now they are taken away from me."

"Bookends! What are you talking about?" Abbey asked.

Doug turned to her. "Bookends are what we used to call kids, you know, when you had a son and a daughter. A pair of bookends."

Abbey just stared at him. "Baby, I know how much you loved those children, I wish this would have not happened. If there is anyone on this planet who deserved children to love, you are the one. You spent all your time with them and did anything they wanted you to do. Instead of them being spoiled, I think you are the one that was spoiled."

Doug looked down at the floor and began rubbing his hands together. He started to speak, then stopped. Abbey knew he was trying to find the words for exactly what he wanted to say.

He rubbed his face with his hands, drying the tears from his eyes, trying to say the words he wanted to say, but his thoughts could not be put into words. He hesitated, then stood up and quietly left the room. Abbey waited for a while then walked out after him. She found him out in the backyard next to the pool.

"I keep thinking that this is just a dream and that they are going to walk through that door, but that is not going to happen, is it? They are never coming back, are they?"

Abbey grabbed him and hugged him tightly. "No baby, they are not coming back… they are gone."

WHOSE FAULT?

After a moment, Doug stood up. "I have to go down to the church and retrieve my gown and take it to the cleaners. Would you like to join me?"

"No, I am going to go in and relax. We'll talk when you return." Abbey walked into the house and moved a few dishes around and then sat down.

Tilting her head, she had a thought. She made her way to Julia's room. She cracked the door slowly and walked into the room. She paused in the middle of the room and slowly scanned around, taking in Julia's personality. Breathing it in. She walked over to her dresser and looked at the mirror. She grabbed Julia's favorite earrings then began reminiscing what Julia said. "I am not going to take these earrings to Auntie Beth's house because I don't want to accidentally leave them." Abbey looked behind her, then slowly turned around and headed for the bed.

She sat down and began rubbing the comforter, grabbed one of the pillows and put it up to her face. She looked up to the sky and thought, *it still smells like you, baby.* She grabbed another pillow and smelled that one too. Abbey gently put the pillows back on the bed and headed for the closet. She opened the door and walked inside, she reached for a jacket and then a dress and then some blouses.

She fell to her knees and touched all the shoes that were not in boxes. She looked up and noticed a dress that really reminded her of Julia.

"I remember this one," she said to herself. She looked to the ceiling. *This is the one that you were christened in, you were so afraid of being up in front of the church alone you asked me to join you. You were absolutely beautiful in this dress. I had to tell all the boys at the church when it let out that you were too young, and you got upset with me. Your daddy grabbed your arm and made you get into the car just as soon as he got outside of the church.*

CHAPTER 12

"Do you remember that?" Abbey began shaking her head. "My baby, I am sorry that I was not there with you, I wish I had been there with you, my gosh, how I miss talking to you."

Abbey closed the closet door and walked towards the door leading out of the room; she turned around just as she arrived and gave one last look at everything, then walked out.

Doug arrived home and looked around for Abbey. He found her sitting in the backyard.

"Are you alright?"

"Yes," she said and exhaled.

"What was that for? That didn't sound like you had a good day at all."

"Well, today, I tried to go into Julia's room and start boxing her stuff up, but all I could do was think about her with everything I touched. I don't know if I am going to be able to do this."

"Do what?" Doug asked as he pulled up a chair.

Abbey looked at him. "Doug, someone is going to have to clean out their rooms and I don't know if I can do that. I don't even know if I want to live here in this house anymore without them. I keep thinking that I hear one of their voices. When the door opens, I think it's one of them. There is nothing like the disappointment of it not being one of them. Even though I know that it's not possible."

"Me too," Doug said. "I remember the other day when I went into Chris' room, it wasn't comfortable at all. There was just so much to that young man, and you really look past all that stuff until you have to make sense of it."

"I know, even after a few days, I still can't go in there and start taking his stuff out of there, let alone hers."

"What if we hired someone to come in here and take their clothes and things out?" Doug suggested.

Abbey looked away for a while and then looked back at Doug. She looked away again and then back to Doug. "I don't know if that is what I would like. I mean, it is our job no matter how hard it's going to be, and it's going to be very hard."

Doug just listened as she poured out her pain.

"I understand I was just throwing that out there as an option, it's nothing I'd really considered," he said.

"I'll tell you what. Tomorrow we are both going into those rooms and begin cleaning up. Baby steps."

The next morning, Pastor Andrew knocked on the door early. Doug walked to the door, slowly clearing his mind of the night's dream.

He peeked out and then opened the door. "Good morning." He rubbed the sleep from his eyes.

"It's a good morning indeed," Pastor Andrews said. "I was just in the neighborhood and figured I would come and see how you two were doing."

"Uh, it's early," Doug said with a small grin.

"Yes, it is, this is the best time to do God's work."

Doug invited him in and offered some coffee. Abbey heard the men talking and came out to greet the visitor.

"Well, good morning, Mrs. Campbell, what a wonderful morning this is."

Abbey looked at him, eyebrows furrowed. "Is there something wrong?" she quickly asked.

"Not at all. I just come by to see the both of you. We had a very good service last night. Our thoughts were with this family. We prayed and worshiped with you in mind. I hope what happened has not depleted your faith in God."

Abbey walked in from the kitchen with two cups of coffee. "What did you say?"

CHAPTER 12

"I dearly hope that you have not given up on God," he reiterated.

Doug looked at Abbey, Abbey glanced back and then to Pastor Andrews. Doug sat his coffee down then sat down, looking at the floor. He gathered himself, looked around the room until he came back around to Abbey.

"This has come full circle," Doug said. "First of all, we lose our children, and then we tried to cope with that loss, at the same time looking for some understanding. We have struggled with this from day one, looking to fuss with anyone who would want to listen. My marriage was tested from all of this. We argued about faults knowing deep down inside that no one here was at fault. We did something that we had agreed to do before and would probably do again if this had not happened. But the brutal outcome tested our resolve. I have listened to and read scriptures, talked to you and to my wife. We received a rude awakening from family members." He chuckled. "And now we still have one last test."

Pastor Andrews sat down on the couch. "What last test?"

Abbey waited to see if Doug was going to answer, but when he was slow to say anything, she answered. "We still have to find the strength to go into their bedrooms and box up their belongings."

Pastor Andrews's eyes grew wide, knowing the pain that was going to be associated with that. "Would you like to say a small prayer before performing that very difficult task?"

Doug looked at Pastor Andrews. "So, you want me to say a prayer and ask God for the strength? You want me to ask God for what? Helping with the cleanup process of something He has taken from me? Right now, I don't know if I can do that. I am only human with human thoughts and this is the hardest thing that I have ever had to do."

WHOSE FAULT?

Doug stood up and walked closer to Abbey. "Ecclesiastic folks only see one way when the pain is not their own."

"Honestly, Pastor, would you be ready to pray if this set of circumstances were your own?"

"Doug, Abbey, I could never understand your pain and what it is taken for you and your wife to muster up the courage to continue through life. I am sure it is sometimes unbearable or has been. But you must revisit your faith. You mustn't let go of your beliefs."

Pastor Andrews stood up and walked towards the door. "Trust is the hardest thing to do, and faith is the strong or unshakeable belief in something, especially without proof or evidence. I have to go right now, but I will revisit you soon." He gave one last look at them and then let himself out of the house.

Abbey looked at Doug. "What was that about?"

"The church regularly reaches out to help, but they should ask instead of just prying."

Abbey walked away, then stopped. "Doug, do you want breakfast?"

"Not now, I just want to relax for a bit. Calm my inner self." He walked to the bedroom and lay back on the bed.

Abbey began opening the curtains and letting the sunshine into the house. She began thinking of the job ahead, the daunting task of touching and memories, everything in their rooms had memories attached to them. She slowly took a sip of her coffee, turned on the television and laid back in the recliner chair.

She was interrupted by the doorbell ringing. When she opened the door, there was a young lady waiting on the porch.

"May I help you?"

"Oh hi, Mrs. Campbell, my name is Estelle, is Julia home?"

Abbey stood completely still, staring at the girl.

CHAPTER 12

Estelle chatted on, not noticing the frozen look on Abbey's face. "I've been on vacation for the last month and just got back home. We are supposed to go to the mall and window shop for school clothes."

Estelle waited without saying anything. She just smiled.

Abbey finally invited her in and waited for Estelle to sit down. Abbey walked back to the recliner and again looked at Estelle.

"Is there something wrong, Mrs. Campbell?"

Abbey put both her hands together and placed her face in them. "Yes, dear. I'm afraid there is."

Estelle's face went from smiley to serious.

"Julia is not here," Abbey's voice squeaked out.

Doug walked into the living room still in his pajamas. He stopped when he noticed Estelle.

"Doug, meet Estelle," Abbey introduced them. "She came here looking for Julia."

He looked at her, blinking in confusion.

"You see, she's been out of town for a while and just got back. She came to go to the mall with Julia."

Doug waited for a while and then sat down at the table.

"Did you see those flowers out on the lawn?" Abbey asked. "I know they are kind of dying off out there."

Estelle turned to the window, and then turned back with her hand over her mouth.

Abbey hesitated. "Julia was in an airplane crash with her brother. It happened a week ago. The funeral was just Saturday."

Estelle's face was full of tears as she turned and looked back out the window, groping for understanding.

Doug walked over and gave Estelle some tissues. Abbey walked over and sat with her, but Estelle couldn't stop the flow of tears. "Julia was... my best friend... she was the best friend

WHOSE FAULT?

I could have, and I didn't know. I didn't even get to go to her... funeral to say goodbye." She spoke between sobs.

Both ladies began to hug and cry. Doug grabbed the box of tissues and brought it to them.

Abbey waited for Estelle to collect herself. "I am sorry. I know this is not what you expected when you decided to come here."

Estelle waited for a while, grabbed the last tissue she held in her hand and wiped the last of the tears in her eyes. She stood up and looked at both of them. "I am very sorry for your loss. Julia was very special and very popular at the school. I am going to miss her something awful." She walked back to Abbey and gave her a hug and then over to Doug and gave him a hug. Slowly, she walked to the door, then stopped. "Can I please have the address where you laid Julia to rest? I want to go and talk to her and also say goodbye."

"Of course," Abbey said. She grabbed an obituary off the mantel and handed it to her. Estelle looked at the obituary and said *thanks* and walked out the door.

Doug walked back to the bedroom, and Abbey headed for the kitchen. She looked out the window at the flowers when she noticed Beth and Nathan pull into the driveway.

Beth opened the door and walked into the house.

"I saw you through the window," Beth said and continued to the couch.

Abbey stared at her from the entrance of the kitchen. Beth stared back, waiting for some kind of response.

"Well..." Beth said looking serious.

Abbey stood silently looking out at her. A single tear began to well up, then fall from her face as she just stood.

"I never left the city," Beth said. "There was no way that I could leave you in your time of need. I stayed away long enough

CHAPTER 12

for you and Doug to communicate what was going on in your thoughts."

"First of all,... wait," Abbey said. "Please wait."

She walked over and sat down next to Beth. "Thank you, Sis."

Doug walked out dressed and was surprised to see Beth sitting in the room. He stopped in his tracks. He looked at Abbey and then at Beth.

"Hello, Doug," Beth said, breaking the silence.

Doug whispered *hello,* feeling embarrassed. He went to the couch and gave Beth a hug. "You have no idea how happy I am to see you here in this house."

Nathan knocked lightly on the door, walked in, and gave Doug a handshake. Nathan looked at Abbey. "We stayed at the hotel down the street. We talked to the pastor the other day and then just waited until we thought was the best time to return here."

"Every day that went by, I wanted to come over here," Beth said. "But I knew you two needed time alone... together. Have you two had time to talk about, umm, *things*?" She put a strong emphasis on the last word.

"Yes, we have," Doug said. "We've talked about this and other things concerning this whole... situation. What we have found out is that we are both in deep pain. But we also realize that we both are parents and should talk and do things together concerning our kids. Right now, we are working on how to go to their bedrooms and start the cleaning up process."

"Oh. Let me get this off my chest first. I'm sorry for barging into your home like I did," Beth said. "What I said was completely out of line and not for me to say. After we checked into the hotel, Nathan and I talked about what happened here. He made me understand that with what was going on, I should have been more sensitive to your feelings."

"No, I think what you said needed to be said," Abbey said. "We both needed to hear that. And coming from you made it more significant. Our pastor told us that you had visited him and wanted him to come and talk to us. I really appreciate what you said and did," Abbey said, reaching for another hug.

"Well," Beth said, standing up. "Now that all that is done, and we are a family again, is there anything you need for us to do?"

Abbey looked into Beth's eyes. "I would love for you to be by my side going into Julia's room. This is going to be very hard for me and I need my big sister to be there for me and with me."

"That is not a problem, and when we are finished, we will also do Chris' room." She looked at the men. "We would sure appreciate it if you would involve yourselves in this."

Nathan walked over to Doug and put his hand on Doug's shoulder. "I will be right by your side, man."

After about an hour, Doug walked out of the room and stuck his head back in, "Does anyone want some water?"

Abbey and Beth answered. "Yes, please."

Nathan walked out and went with Doug.

The men walked into the kitchen, Nathan opened the refrigerator and grabbed four bottles of water. "Hey man," Doug yelled, "Come and see this."

Nathan put the bottles of water on the kitchen counter and walked over to Doug, standing in the living room looking out the front window.

Looking out the window, he saw people working in the front yard, replacing wilted flowers with fresh flowers at the center of the *Makeshift Memorial*.

Doug yelled for Abbey and Beth to come to the window.

"What is it?" Abbey asked as she approached.

Doug continued waving for her to come to the window and see for herself.

CHAPTER 12

Beth and Abbey arrived at the same time. Beth grabbed Abbey as she put her hand over her mouth and started heavily crying and went weak. Beth tried to find a place to sit Abbey.

Beth walked over and helped Abbey into a chair. They waited a few moments to give Abbey a chance to recover. "You better now?" Beth asked.

Abbey nodded. So, the four of them walked to the door and out on the porch. All the neighbors were bringing flowers and putting them next to two large photos of Julia and Chris.

Pastor Andrews, the church choir, the ushers and some of the congregation were there, spearheading the event.

When Pastor Andrews saw the four of them come out of the house, he walked over to greet them. "What a beautiful day in the Lord," he said.

Abbey and Doug just stared at him questioningly.

"Is there something wrong?" Pastor Andrews asked.

Doug tried to say something but was so surprised and choked up by what was going on. He couldn't get out a word.

Abbey just held on to Beth tighter as she watched friends and neighbors bringing flowers and cards. Beth motioned for Abbey to walk off the porch so that they could greet everyone and see the pictures placed in the center of the yard.

Estelle came over to greet Abbey. She waved. "Hello, Mrs. Campbell."

Pastor Andrews walked over with Doug and Nathan to where Estelle, Beth, and Abbey were. "This is a remarkable young lady," he said, looking at Estelle. "She is the one who made this happen. She came to the church and asked for me, but I wasn't there, so she talked to my wife and waited until I returned. She told us that she wasn't here for the funeral and had really just found out about what happened. She also felt bad about not being able to attend the funeral and wanted to get fresh flowers for the memorial, but when she went to purchase them, she didn't have enough money. My, aren't florists getting expensive. But I digress. She stopped by the church to see if there was something we could do to help her out. She told us about what she wanted to do and there was no way that we could *not* be a part of this. After she told us, she took it upon herself to go door to door to all of your neighbors and asked if they could join in this ceremony. They, of course, obliged and this is the result of her diligent work. I just *know* the Lord is pleased with you today, Estelle."

Abbey looked at Estelle, her eyes filled with wonder. "Thank you. We really appreciate what you've done. I-I can't seem to express what this…" she took a moment to even her breathing. "What this means to us. It is beyond kindness."

All the neighbors came over to greet the family and pay their respects.

CHAPTER 13

One month later

Abbey walked out of the bedroom looking for Doug. She had slept in and awoken to an empty bed. She looked all around the house and then finally in the back yard.

She went back to the kitchen to put on a pot of coffee, but the coffee had already been made. As she was reaching for cups, she looked out the window. There was Doug in the front yard, cleaning out the old dead flowers and taken the pictures down.

She knocked on the window and waved to him, he put the shovel down and walked to the house.

"Good morning," he said. "There is a fresh pot of coffee. I figured you would like some when you finally got out of bed."

Abbey smiled. "My first day back to work sure took a lot out of me. I am sore all over."

Doug laughed. "Lady, all you do is sit at a desk."

She poked him on the arm playfully. He walked over to get a cup of coffee. Abbey watched as he grabbed a cup that they both knew was cracked and leaked at the bottom. She watched him as he started pouring, waiting for him to react to the hot coffee leaking onto his hand.

As he poured, he smiled at her. "Something amiss, dear?"

Abbey just laughed and shook her head as the hot coffee made him realize that he had the cracked cup. Abbey laughed and threw him a towel and walked out of the kitchen. "When you are finished cleaning up the mess you've just made, you can go finish the front yard." She laughed all the way back to the bedroom. A few minutes later, Doug entered and stood next to her. "It is so wonderful to see you laughing and trying to enjoy yourself again."

"Yeah, the kids gave me so much joy and also had me so busy that just being me was something I had put on the back burner until they were out of school and on their own."

"I understand," Doug said. "Now that we no longer have them, we have to find something to substitute the time without them. Well, I am going to finish cleaning the yard then go and get my suit out of the cleaners. We are going to church tomorrow, right?"

Abbey sat silently and then agreed. "Yes, we are going back to church. For a moment, I didn't think that I would ever say that again."

"I know what you mean," Doug said then walked out to go finish the front yard.

The Campbells walked into the church the next morning as the choir was singing a hymn. Pastor Andrews stood up as they began to walk down the aisle to find a seat. One of the Ushers noticed the Pastor looking for someone to seat them in the front row. The church grew silent as the entire congregation acknowledged the Campbell's presence. Joyful hand clapping and shouts of "Praise the Lord" rang out in the church.

"Hallelujah," Pastor Andrews said as the Campbells sat down.

CHAPTER 13

One of the ushers walked over to Doug and invited him to join the other deacons sitting in the pew.

When Doug stood up and started the long walk to the pew, he looked around at the congregation, especially at Abbey. He started having flashbacks of Julia and Chris, and then he began thinking of what he'd talked about with the Pastor and his wife.

Pastor Andrews finished the morning sermon and asked that everyone stay for a few minutes. He asked Doug, Abbey, and Estelle to come to the front of the church.

Everyone clapped as the three of them stood and looked out to the congregation. Pastor Andrews walked in front of them and praised them then turned to the church.

"I know God is an awesome God. I know He hears and sees everything, and I know He seen what these fine people were going through. He knows of their pain. He knows of how much they loved their children. Friends, please, whatever you do when things seem to be going the wrong way, always get up again! Always confess up again! Always pray up again! Always live up again! Always look up again! Now let me leave you with this last scripture. *'If you have fallen, do not lean on your own understanding.'* Proverbs 3:5-6. *Do not rationalize, repent.* James 4:7-8, *'Resist the devil. Draw nigh to God.'* In order to draw nigh, you must be away. Now everyone here, go on out and have a blessed and great week."

"The End"

www.ingramcontent.com/pod-product-compliance
Ingram Content Group UK Ltd.
Pitfield, Milton Keynes, MK11 3LW, UK
UKHW022223230426
12048UKWH00016BA/1025